ENEMIES ALL AROUND

The room was now a babble of excited, angry voices. A low growl came from the throat of sullen, square-faced Jess Armstrong. The man stood hunched a little, as though only waiting a signal to attack. Walt thought unbelievingly: *This isn't possible! It can't be happening!*

But it was happening. These men, his friends and neighbors, had turned against him. In their faces he saw a number of things, none of which was pleasant. He saw hatred, dislike, suspicion, and distrust. And he saw something else, which disturbed him more than all the rest—a kind of eagerness. Suddenly he knew they wanted to destroy him. They wanted to destroy Ramrod.

GUNS OF VENGEANCE

LEWIS B. PATTEN

LEISURE BOOKS **NEW YORK CITY**

LEISURE BOOKS ®

July 2004

Published by special arrangement with Golden West Literary Agency.

Dorchester Publishing Co., Inc.
200 Madison Avenue
New York, NY 10016

"Death Fans This Gun" first appeared in *Ace-High Western Stories* (9/54).

ISBN 0-8439-5376-4

Printed in the United States of America.

Visit us on the web at www.dorchesterpub.com.

GUNS OF
VENGEANCE

Table of Contents

Death
Fans This Gun

Pride got Ed Mallory out of his bed. The sun had been up for three hours, and all three of them had been hours of wakeful torment for Ed. Behind him was a lifetime of rising with the dawn. But now he was old and weak, and it hurt him to move.

He learned the easy ways, the effortless ways of doing things. Ed eased himself to the side of the bed. He dropped his feet to the floor and sat up. He waited a moment until the dizziness went away, and then he got to his feet.

He was like a wraith in his faded red-flannel underwear. With a pronounced and painful limp, he crossed the shabby room and took his trousers from the back of a chair. Leaning against the wall, he put them on. His movements were slow and careful and occasionally jerky. But none of the pain he was feeling showed on his face.

It was a face seamed with sun and weather, an indomitable old face, like granite upon which frost and time, rain and wind, had done their work. A long, white knife scar ran along his ribs on the right side. There was a bulge of proud flesh and scar tissue between neck and left shoulder where a bullet had entered and lodged long ago. There were other scars, not showing, and these were his medals. They told of the high points in his life; they told of his pride and his profession.

Sitting down in the chair, he pulled on his boots. He was breathing harshly now from exertion, but he got them on and, after waiting a few moments, stood up again.

Out the back door he went, into the bright spring sunshine. He put a bucket under the pump spout and worked the handle until it was half full. He carried it back into the house, poured part of it into a rusty wash pan. He washed his face, wryly considering the stubble of white whiskers in the cracked and peeling mirror.

He put on his shirt and started for the front door. With his hand on the knob, he turned and looked at the stove. There was wood in the box outside, and it wouldn't take long to start a fire. With the fire started, it wouldn't take much effort to put on a pot of coffee. He opened the door and stepped out onto his tiny porch.

The house was an old, one-room affair, wedged tightly between the Northern Hotel and Burkhardt's Mercantile. It had a bare, tiny front yard and a sagging picket fence that had once been white. There were a couple of loose boards on the porch that the old man had to watch, but he did this from long habit and sank into his rocker with a sigh of relief.

The house faced west, so he now sat in cool and fragrant shade. A lilac bush bloomed at the corner of the porch. Two giant cottonwoods grew in the yard, and their leaves rustled audibly in the breeze.

The old man felt guilty about breakfast. He really wasn't hungry, and it took a bit of effort to fix himself a meal. But his guilt remained. He had the feeling that if he could only eat a good, hearty breakfast each morning, perhaps he could rebuild his strength.

The rocker *creaked* as it moved back and forth. A farmer with a load of produce in his wagon drove past leisurely. A cowpuncher from Two Bar, out on the mesa, showing the signs of a night-long celebration, rode a jogging horse northward through the dry, cool dust of the shaded street. Downstreet, toward the livery stable, the old man could hear the steady ring of a blacksmith's hammer against an anvil. Farther away, at the edge of town, the seven o'clock passenger train hooted and puffed noisily out of the station.

Ed Mallory grinned as he saw a black cat start across the street and he bet himself that the cat wouldn't make it unobserved. He won. A shaggy white collie came off the verandah of the Northern Hotel with stiff-legged jumps, barking furiously.

The cat scooted across and disappeared under the latticed porch of Lucy Carroway's dressmaking shop. The dog stopped in mid-street. He looked at the old man, wagged his tail apologetically, and trotted back to resume his wait for his master.

Three horsemen entered the town from the north. They rode along Main, right down the middle. The old man drew the glance of the youngest one, who said something to his companions and reined over to the sagging fence. He dismounted, nudged open the gate with his boot, and came up the hard-packed walk.

The old man gave the young man's two companions a long, thoughtful glance before he turned his attention to his visitor, who said: "You look good this morning, Ed. Had your breakfast?"

Ed Mallory nodded, lying. "Appetite's going away, though," he said. "I don't get much exercise." He put his deep-set eyes on the younger man's hard, reckless face. Without seeming to, he looked at the wide, muscular shoulders, at the flat, hard belly, the long thighs. He looked at the sagging gun belt, at the holstered, single-action Colt revolver. He asked: "Who're your friends, Will?"

Will shrugged. "Drifters. Passing through." His eyes failed to hold Ed Mallory's. They were eyes that nurtured a lot of bitterness. Ed Mallory remembered that there had always been that deep-hidden bitterness in Will Kostka, even when he'd been a boy.

Well, why not? His father had been a drunk, his mother a slattern. He'd gotten nothing from the town but snubs and insults as long as he could remember. *I saw you playing with that Kostka brat this afternoon. Stay away from him, you hear? Stay away from him or I'll take a razor strop to you.*

At fourteen, Will had been almost man-size, a brooding, somber boy, a boy whose eyes showed his hatred and contempt for the town. They were afraid of him, distrustful. He grew up virtually alone.

He'd reminded Ed of himself when he'd been that age. Ed's eyes stared off into emptiness, remembering.

Will said: "You need anything, Ed?"

"No." Ed shook his head, coming back. He noticed that the two Will had been with were dismounting before the saloon, far down the street. He didn't like their looks. He had an uneasy feeling about them. That was his years as sheriff of Blanco County working on him. And there had been something about Will's tone.

Ed asked: "What d'you mean, do I need anything? You going away?"

"Well, I might." Will fished in his pocket for tobacco. He shaped a cigarette with elaborate care.

"Why?"

"Why not?" Will suddenly twisted the carefully made cigarette between his fingers. The tobacco spilled to the ground. He looked at Ed Mallory, frowning. "What has this damned town ever done for me? Why should I stay here? Except for you, there isn't a man in town I can call my friend. There isn't a girl or a woman that'll go to a Saturday night dance with me. I thought I was all right. I had a job at Two Bar, but they laid me off last night."

"Why?"

14

Will Kostka shrugged. "Same old story. Hard times. Cattle prices falling. Got to cut expenses. But I'm the one to go." Resentment blazed in his eyes. "I've been a good hand for Two Bar, Ed."

Ed said: "I'll miss you, Will. You riding out with those two drifters?"

Will toed the dirt. "Maybe. I don't know yet. You sure you don't need anything?"

Ed shook his head. He had a little money saved, enough to eat one meal a day at the Northern Hotel. He noticed that Will was getting fidgety, so he said: "See me again before you go, Will."

"Sure, Ed." With apparent relief, Will went down the walk. He flashed one of his rare smiles at the old man as he rode away.

Ed's chin sank onto his chest and he went on rocking, rocking. He was thinking back. There was no place else for his mind to go any more. There wasn't anything ahead, so his mind went back.

He'd been sheriff of Blanco County for thirty years. He'd been a lonesome man, always a lonesome man. There had only been one woman for him, and that had been when he was young. He could still remember her, could see her bright, quick smile as though he had last seen it yesterday instead of twenty-five years before.

Being sheriff had been a dangerous job then. Blanco County and the town of Blanco had attracted a lot of the riff-raff that got squeezed out of Lincoln County, that got run out of Tombstone. Things had tamed down as the years passed, but there was still need for a sheriff—an active one, not an old, crippled one.

The chair *squeaked* gently. Children ran along the street on their way to school, their voices young and eager. They

15

were like puppies, playing, scuffling. The old man smiled. They stopped coming, but still he could hear their voices, mingling in high confusion as they played in the schoolyard. The bell rang, and the shrill yelling stopped.

Ed Mallory had wanted a son, but Ellen had died giving him one. The baby had died, too. It left a void in Ed's life. When Will Kostka's father got run over by a freight train, his mother had skipped town, leaving the boy. It worried the town, but Ed Mallory took him in and raised him. Ed Mallory frowned at his thoughts. Maybe some of Will's trouble could be traced to Ed Mallory. Maybe he'd made a mistake.

Ed had known only one trade, the gun and the star that adorned his vest. He taught Will Kostka the gun, patiently, over the long years. He tried to teach Will about the star, too, but the town interfered with that. They wouldn't let Will Kostka believe what Ed Mallory believed, that men and women everywhere were essentially kind and good. Will would never accept the idea that they were worth protecting and defending, even at the risk of a man's life. The townspeople made Will hate and despise them.

Suddenly the old man caught the aroma of coffee drifting from the hotel kitchen on the light breeze. He hobbled down the walk and out the rickety gate, turning toward the Northern. He wished he'd taken the time to shave this morning.

The Northern was only next door, but old Ed was tired when he got there. He went into the big dining room and sat down close to the door. Molly Ribault came toward him, smiling.

She asked: "Celebrating, Ed?" She was a tall, dark-haired girl, slim and well-made. Ed wasn't too old to notice that. He liked her.

He looked puzzled for a moment, but then he said: "Oh,

the coffee? I smelled it brewing over on my porch and it smelled good. Get me a cup, will you, Molly?"

"Sure." She touched his thin shoulder fondly. Her eyes showed pity, but Ed didn't see that. He was staring at his thin, blue-veined hands on the table before him. The skin was speckled brown, as shiny and transparent as old parchment. He flexed the right hand, let it drop to rub the place where the holster used to ride. He began to worry about Will and his two strange friends.

Molly brought the coffee, then pulled out a chair and sat down across from him. She said: "You're worried about something, Ed. Can I help?"

Ed murmured: "It's Will. Two Bar laid him off and he's leaving. You can't help, Molly. You tried that once."

She had. She'd gone with Will in open defiance of the town. She'd liked Will. Maybe she'd have loved him once she got under his shell of bitterness and resentment. But her father had stopped Will on the street one day. He'd called Will things no man should have to take and Will had taken them. He hadn't seen Molly after that except for a cold nod once in a while on the street.

Molly put her warm, young hand over Ed's cold one. "Don't worry about Will, Ed. He'll be all right. Maybe a new town where he isn't known. Maybe that will help him."

Ed nodded. Molly, paler, got up to wait on another customer. Ed finished his coffee, and started to get up. A man laid a hand on his shoulder, then moved over to sink into the chair across from him. Sheriff Tate. A tall, thin man with a thin, harsh face. A good man. Too hard, maybe, too quick and harsh in his judgments, but a good man.

The sheriff, grinning, said: "Ed, I need another deputy. You real sure you wouldn't want to come out of retirement and help me out?"

It was a joke between them and Ed tried to smile. This morning, it didn't seem like a joke. He wished he could go back a few years. The star and the gun. He wished he still wore them.

He said: "I'm getting too old, Sheriff. Too old."

Tate smiled and started to leave. Ed put out a hand and stopped him. "Sheriff, do you really need a deputy?"

Tate looked surprised, puzzled. "Ed, I was just kidding. But as a matter of fact, I do need a man. Sam Pratt took the marshal's job down at Stillwater. You know someone?"

Ed's eyes were beseeching. "Sheriff, how about Will?"

Tate stood up, embarrassed. "Ed, I can't. The town wouldn't stand for it. Besides. . . ."

Ed muttered: "All right, Sheriff. Forget it."

The sheriff went out, hurrying, glad to get away. Ed put a nickel down on the table. He got up and limped back through the lobby to the verandah.

Almost all of the street was now sun-washed. Ed stood in the sun, letting its warmth soak into his frail old bones. He got out his old curve-stemmed pipe and carefully packed it full. Holding it in his yellowed teeth, he puffed it alight. Smoking, he went back along the walk and turned in at his gate.

He felt better for the coffee and the pipe. The chair protested as he sank into it. Downstreet, Will's horse and those of the two drifters were racked together before the saloon. The morning dragged past, and the old man dozed.

Ed Mallory always waited till the noon rush was over before he went into the hotel for his dinner. He didn't like to be any bother, and Molly Ribault was pretty busy between twelve and twelve-thirty. Across the street, the bank door opened and Silas McFee, pompous and black-clad, crossed the street to the Northern. His cashier, who was also his son-in-law, came out shortly afterward and turned uptown toward home.

Merchants came from their shops all along the street, some heading for the Northern and some for home. After a while, the street was deserted.

The old man started to doze again, but movement far down the street caught his eye and jerked him awake. Will and the two drifters mounted their horses and rode abreast up the street. At the corner, the drifters peeled away to wait, and Will came on.

He ground-tied his horse at the gate and came up the packed dirt walk. "Well, I'm going, Ed." He came onto the porch and put his hand toward Ed. Will kept glancing back toward the corner where his two companions waited. When he released Ed's hand, his own hand dropped and absently loosened his Colt in its holster.

These were signs and Ed had been sheriff for a long time. He said—"Get a new start somewhere, Will."—yet there was no real hope in him. He'd had Will to mold, but the town had undone everything he'd tried to do. Talk wouldn't change things now.

Will nodded and turned to go. He hesitated, turning back then. The bitterness was momentarily gone from his eyes. He said: "Ed, I owe you an awful lot. I wanted you to know that I know it."

He was gone then, quickly, striding toward his horse with his back stiff and straight. The gun rode high on his thigh, moving with his own movement.

Ed Mallory got up and went into the house. He looked at the bed. He was tired and he was hungry. But mostly he was tired. This was the end of a lot of things, and no one could change or stop it. He'd be hearing the shots soon and

19

he didn't want to hear them. Because then he'd know that there was no turning around for Will.

He thought about that for a moment. He'd done all he. . . . Suddenly he was moving—faster than he'd moved in a long, long time. He opened the closet door and got down the gun and belt. He buckled them on and started for the door. He halted, hesitated, and then went back to the old, scratched gray dresser. The star was in the top drawer. It was tarnished almost black. Ed rubbed it against his sleeve, and then pinned it to his shirt.

Almost brisk was his step as he went out the door, down the walk, and through the gate. The three horses were just around the corner from the bank and one of the strangers was holding them. Ed knew he'd made no mistake. He crossed the street, wanting to hurry, but fearing to. He couldn't afford one of his weak spells now.

He reached the far side of the street, breathing hard. Not more than a dozen yards remained. He went along the walk and stepped carefully into the bank.

It was dark in here compared to the street and it took him an instant before his eyes accustomed themselves to it. There was a big, tile-floored room in front of the cages that led back to the office of Silas McFee. A scared, gray-haired woman stood behind one of the cage grills with her hands in the air. An equally scared man stood beside the gate, outside of it. Will, gun in hand, stood facing them with his back to Ed and the door. Ed, moving cautiously, had made no sound.

The other drifter came from the rear of the bank, carrying a couple of sacks. He looked at Ed, shifted his gun so that it pointed at Ed. He said: "Careful, old man. Turn around. Then unbuckle that belt and let it drop." He laughed and spoke directly to Will.

"This town must like their lawmen old. A good wind would easily blow that one over."

Ed could see Will's back muscles go tense. He said: "I tried to tell you about the star, Will."

Will turned around. He looked at Ed with eyes that were suddenly scared. Ed touched the star with his left hand as though he found reassurance in it. Will's glance swiveled quickly to the drifter, and back again.

The drifter's eyes were getting hot and impatient. "Do like I said, old man!" His voice was sure.

Ed knew what was coming. Instinctively he braced himself for it because it was going to hurt. His hand started for his gun, but it had been too long. The slowness of age and weakness was obviously evident in him.

Will didn't hesitate even a fraction of a second. He made his choice as though it were really no choice at all. And the old man's patient teaching had not been in vain. Ed saw the drifter's eyes narrow as his finger tightened down on the trigger. Will was faster. His gun came around and belched its cloud of smoke and flame. The sound filled the room and poured through the open door into the street that was especially quiet now.

The drifter's eyes widened slightly, and then the force of the bullet tearing into his breastbone drove him backward and down to the floor. There was a moment of utter silence. Will slid his smoking gun back into its holster.

Still silence.

From the street came a shout and the pound of a horse's hoofs. Ed made a tight smile. "Every man for himself." His gun was in his hand. He shoved it back into its holster.

The woman in the cage turned white. The man beside the cage put his face down into his hands, shaking. The woman came out and both of them came toward Ed timidly.

21

The man, Hiram Harper, said in a shaking voice: "Ed, that took a lot of courage."

Ed shook his head. "No. What Will did took a lot of courage. Why don't you people in this town give him a chance?" he asked.

Will's voice was bitter, his laugh harsh: "You're wasting your breath, Ed. This is what they've been waiting for . . . the chance to say . . . 'He was never any good. I knew he'd come to a bad end.' "

Hiram Harper did not seem to hear Will. He asked, still staring at Ed: "What do you want, Ed?"

Ed swallowed. "I want you to say that Will was with me. Is that a lot to ask?" He was very unsure inside, but his craggy old face didn't show that.

Harper stumbled, lowering his glance. "I guess it isn't, Ed. What do you think, Bessie?"

The color had reached to Bessie's face. There was sharp asperity in her voice. "I think this town owes a lot to Ed. I think it's got to make up to Will. I think it's about time somebody really started doing it."

Sheriff Tate, out of breath and red of face, came into the bank on a run. Tiredness ran through Ed. His forehead glistened with a light film of perspiration. He wanted to sit down, but he had to get across the street before he could. He went out the door, hearing Tate's sharp questions ringing in his ears. He felt a little like smiling now as he walked very straight.

Tate had said that he needed a deputy, and Will knew about the gun. Now, maybe, he'd get a solid chance to learn about the star.

Guns of
Vengeance

Chapter One

Horse and rider moved like a speck across the empty immensity of land, across sagebrush flat, through shaded quakie pocket, and at last through the fringe of dark spruce that guarded the precipitous rim. Here Rand halted, his eyes noting the sorrel hide of his horse with its thin coating of mud caused by mingling sweat and dust. In his nostrils was the sour-hot smell of the horse, the strong, pitchy smell of spruce, and the tangy, wild smell of scrub sage crushed under his horse's hoofs. He looked out across the shimmering heat haze in the valley and beyond, toward the purple-shrouded, high slopes of Rampart Mesa, twenty miles southward and across the Roaring Fork River.

He was hot from the merciless, hammering rays of the sun and his mouth was like cotton. Sweat stained the back of his khaki shirt, beaded his upper lip, and gathered on his head under the sweatband of his Stetson. A thin stubble of dark brown whiskers covered his lean, muscled jaw. His blue eyes were brooding as he stuck a hand inside his shirt and scratched his hairy chest. His hand came away wet with perspiration.

The Rands' Double R, or Ramrod brand as folks called it, spread out below him, but there was neither pleasure nor pride in his dark, somber face as he looked down at it. The hayfields showed, instead of the bright green color of healthy, growing hay, a darker, more drab shade that told of the alfalfa's crying need for water and its stunted growth. Blooming already, he thought, and the damned

25

stuff not over a foot high.

Streaks of lighter green ran through it, evidence of an attempt to irrigate it with the meager waters of Wild Horse Creek. Rand had ordered old Mac to concentrate on this rather than try to spread the dwindling supply of water over the entire ranch. Later, if the creek didn't dry up altogether, Mac might get water over another fifty or hundred acres, and that would help. But not much.

An edge of irritation rose in Walt Rand's mind. He looked down at the house and thought: *Damn you, Jake, would Claude have done any better than I have?* His mind said no, Claude wouldn't, but he also knew Jake would never admit it.

Walt tried to deride himself out of his irritability, but somehow failed. It seemed to grow rather than diminish, for behind him now were the two thought-dulling weeks of backbreaking, dawn-to-dark cattle work and ahead was more of his father's peevish nagging, his apparently senseless antagonism. Walt dreaded going home.

He studied the house, almost hidden beneath the spreading arms of the giant cottonwoods. It was like a miniature doll's house at this distance. The horses in the corral looked like ants. Three or four miles away, horizontally, the house was over twenty-five hundred feet below the rim.

Still hesitating, he found a damp sack of tobacco in his shirt pocket and rolled a cigarette. He lit it and dragged the smoke deeply into his lungs.

Then, with an almost invisible shrug, he kneed his horse onto the narrow shelf trail and began his descent. The view of Kenyon's place, above Ramrod, was obscured by an outcropping of rim rock, but he could see the varicolored fields of the smaller ranches below Ramrod reaching all the way to the river. Three other creeks branched off Wild Horse—

Schwartz Creek, Rye Creek, and Little Dry Creek—and all had their complement of dried-up ranches. All were occupied by men growing desperate, facing a winter in which there would be no feed for their stock.

Walt tried to shift his thoughts, to change the pattern of irritability in his mind. *Damn it,* he thought, *it's this heat that makes me feel so sour.* But he knew there was a great deal more to it than that.

There was Claude, Walt's brother, who, even though he was dead, still lived in the house at Ramrod. There was Jake, Walt's father, whose tongue was needle-sharp and continually in use; Jake was never satisfied by anything.

But there was Rose, too. Walt's face softened now as he thought of his wife, and a spark of eagerness was born in his thin, browned face. He let himself think of holding her after two weeks of being away. He felt hunger stir in the depths of his body and unconsciously urged his horse a little faster.

He came around the jutting promontory then and could look above the boundaries of Ramrod to where Nick Kenyon's greasy-sack bachelor spread nestled in the crowding walls of the narrowing cañon. What he saw made him forget Rose. He saw the bright shine of irrigation water spread like a sheet of silver over Kenyon's fields.

Immediately the edginess he had been fighting returned. His eyes narrowed with anger and his mouth compressed. Under his breath he muttered: "Why the dirty son-of-a-bitch! Gone two weeks, and I'll bet the thievin' skunk's had my water thirteen days of it."

Ramrod had the best water rights—in dry years virtually the only water rights—out of Wild Horse Creek. Ramrod had nine second feet of water and the number one right to it, although now there wasn't more than half that much in the creek.

Kenyon's father, on the other hand, had taken up his place after Ramrod was established and the water appropriated. So Kenyon had only flood-water rights to half a second foot, which meant in summer he had nothing unless Ramrod was good enough to share their water with him.

Most of the time they were. Old Jake had always given them water. Claude had given Kenyon water off and on, beginning fifteen years ago when Jake had his stroke and continuing until Claude died last winter. Walt had given Kenyon some water this year, even though giving it meant that Ramrod was even shorter. But Kenyon was never satisfied. He had to steal more.

Dull anger smoldered in Walt as he thought of Kenyon. What ate on a man like that? He wouldn't think of stealing money, or a horse, or cattle. But he'd take every chance he could find to steal water. Walt had come out many a morning to find his own ditches just beginning to run, and seen Kenyon walking toward his house with a shovel over his shoulder.

He'd warned Kenyon often enough, too. Now, by God. . . .

Don't take out on Kenyon all the things that are eating you, he told himself. But the sun beat down, sweat ran on his body, and a deer fly stung him viciously on the back of the neck. Dust rose in choking clouds as his horse slid across the talus slope to the foot of the rim.

His thoughts went on. What was the matter with Mac, the irrigator? Hell, maybe he couldn't stop a bruiser like Kenyon from stealing water, but he could go to the water commissioner. And what about Jake? Why hadn't he done something?

He couldn't be there every second of the time and run things right. Half of Ramrod's work lay atop the great plateau, in summer. There were cattle to be looked after. In dry years like this, at least one out of every ten cattle developed a fungus disease known as hoof rot. They had to be found, roped, and thrown, their infected hoofs painted with caustic.

He abandoned the trail near the bottom of the talus slope for a shorter way straight down, and slid his horse on its haunches to the bottom. Then he put the sorrel into a gallop down through the cedars until he reached the road. All this time, temper kept eating away at his mind.

He saw Mac, bent and old, but peerless with shovel and stream of water, trudging across the fields toward the house, his shovel over his shoulder. Walt got a grip on himself with an effort, reminding himself that Mac's job wasn't to fight for Ramrod's water—it was to spread it over the fields.

He turned his glance toward the house, anticipating his arrival, but somehow dreading it, too. His thoughts of Rose were crowded aside by anger, thinking how old Jake would jump astride him the minute he walked in the door, digging in the verbal spurs.

As he turned in the gate, his eye caught the merest glimpse of a brown horse's rump disappearing into the locusts that fringed the creek behind the house. Now who in hell was that? Kenyon had a brown horse. Walt remembered the way Kenyon had always looked at Rose—the way a stallion looks at a mare in heat.

His temper boiled again. Galloping, he almost went past the house in pursuit of the vanished horseman. But in time good sense overcame angry rashness. He didn't need to worry about Rose. He told himself firmly: *Hell, if it was Kenyon, he was here because he had business here. It just happened he was leaving as I rode in. He wasn't sneaking away.*

He tied his horse to one of the eight-by-eight verandah posts and went into the house. Eagerness rose in him, but a perverse stubbornness made him stifle it.

It was almost as though he were standing off looking at himself and saying: *What the hell's the matter with you? This isn't like you. You're an easy-going guy and always have been. Don't let that god-damn' Kenyon spoil Rose for you. There'll be time enough to take care of him later.*

Rose, having heard the door close, now came into the room, looking questioningly toward it. Whatever doubts Walt may have had were instantly dispelled by the expression on her face, the look a child has glimpsing the Christmas tree on Christmas morning.

She dropped the dishtowel in her hand and ran across the room toward him. Her arms went tightly around his neck, her body tightly against his own. "Walt! Oh, Walt, I'm glad you're home!"

Hunger for her rose in him like a tide. His arms tightened, hurting her, but the tears in her eyes were not from hurt. He lowered his mouth to hers and she responded eagerly. He picked her up in his arms and started for the stairs.

Behind him, he heard the iron tires of old Jake's home-made wheelchair, and heard his father's voice: "Put 'er down, damn you! Ain't no time for lollygaggin' this time of day. There's hell to pay. You seen Mac?"

Rose flushed darkly, pulled out of Walt's arms as he set her down, and went to stand behind the old man's chair, not meeting Walt's eyes. She was a small girl, not yet turned twenty. Her hair was almost black, shining, and tied behind her head today, with a red silk ribbon. Her face was fragile, with high cheek bones, small, firm chin, and full red mouth. She was a sensitive girl, forever being hurt and shamed by Jake's deliberate obscenity.

Walt remembered suddenly the way her face had looked on their wedding night. Jake had made two of the hands carry him upstairs. He'd tied a cowbell to the springs of Walt's bed. Then he talked some of the wedding guests into waiting silently beneath their window.

Walt's face flushed with remembered anger. They'd gone to bed, and the cowbell had set up its awful racket. Walt could still hear the shouted laughter beneath the window, the shouted obscene jests. He could still remember the way Rose's face had looked. God! If he could have found a gun that night. . . .

He looked at his father, coldly angry. How far did a son's duty go? He said: "I saw him crossing the field. Why?"

Jake's great, gaunt frame shook with fury. "Because you ought to talk to him, you stupid fool! Kenyon's got our water!"

Walt stifled his anger with an effort. "I'll get it back."

Jake's voice was filled with bitter, contemptuous sarcasm. "You'll get it back! Can't you get it through your stupid head? Kenyon's got our water for good. He's claimin' it, and that crooked bastard Sidney Bryce is backin' him up."

"What the hell are you talking about?"

Jake sighed disgustedly. "Claude wouldn't have been so god-damn' dumb."

"Claude's dead. Let's leave him that way."

"Hah! Hated him, didn't you? Hated him because he was so damn' much more man than you'll ever be?"

Walt's face reddened, then he caught Rose's beseeching glance on him from behind the old man's chair. He said resignedly: "All right. I'm a dumb bastard and I hated Claude. With that settled, maybe you'll tell me what you're talking about."

"Don't use that tone on me!"

Suddenly Walt's anger boiled. He shouted: "I'll use any damned tone I please! Rose, go get Mac."

Rose hurried from the room, her face stricken. She came back immediately, with Mac shuffling along behind. Walt fought down his anger and tried not to glare at his frightened old irrigator. He asked: "Mac what's this about Kenyon claiming our water?"

"He did, Mister Rand. He did just that. I talked to Bryce today when I went down to complain about Kenyon stealin' water. Bryce said Ramrod's been givin' four and a half feet of water to Kenyon every year for the last thirty years. He says, accordin' to law, givin' water away that long a time means the man it's given to has a right to it. He says Kenyon usin' it and helpin' on the ditch gives him a right that you got to go to court to disprove."

Walt felt as though he'd been kicked in the belly. He was no range lawyer, but he knew a little of water-adjudication laws. Mac was right.

He said: "We never gave Kenyon four and a half feet every year. And he sure as hell didn't do his share on the ditch."

"I know that, Mister Rand. Only we got to prove it."

"All right, Mac. How much water have you got now?"

"None. Kenyon's got the whole damn' creek."

Jake began to rant at Walt, and Mac slunk out the door, small, graying, and bent. Mac was timid as a rabbit and hated being anywhere near Jake.

Walt listened to his father, trying to think, and at last he said irritably: "For God's sake, shut up. And quit worrying. I'll get the water back."

"If you had half the backbone Claude had. . . ."

Walt clenched his fists and glared at his father. *What ate on the old man to make him so god-damn' ornery?* he won-dered. Was it his helplessness after so many years of in-activity? Was it Claude's death? Did he somehow blame himself for that?

Maybe that was it. Maybe the old man thought he'd hounded Claude to his death. Perhaps he had. Certainly Claude had not voluntarily gone up on top of the mountain in a driving blizzard to rescue a bunch of broomtail horses that wasn't worth two hundred dollars. But he'd gone because the old man had nagged and badgered him until he had.

He wished he understood the old man better. It wasn't right for a man to hate his father.

Walt asked, almost desperately: "What was Kenyon doing here just before I rode in?"

The old man cackled nastily. "Layin' down the law to me. The son-of-a-bitch! And smilin' around your loyal wife. I'd say this, boy. You better stick around home more. You'd better stick around or you'll lose more to Kenyon than water."

Walt reached him in a single stride. His big, muscled hands closed on the old man's shirt front. For an instant he stood there, trembling, the veins in his forehead throbbing as though they would burst.

Old Jake's cold blue eyes met his steadily and without fear. They mocked him and dared him to finish what he had begun. It was almost as though Jake were saying: *Go on, boy, go on. Don't stop now. You want to kill me, so why don't you kill me and get it over with?*

Walt released him and stepped away. He realized that his body was bathed in sweat. Rose again stood behind the old man's chair, looking at Walt as though he were some fearful stranger. And yet, somewhere in the depths of her eyes was pity for him, too.

Oddly, her pity angered him almost as much as her fear. He turned and stalked from the room.

He banged through the door and out into the hot sunshine of late afternoon. For an instant he stood on the massive verandah, hearing Jake's cackling, humorless laugh even through the thick log walls of the house.

What's he trying to do to me? he asked himself desperately. *What's he trying to do to Rose?* He considered that, and was honestly surprised at his thought. *Why, damn it, I believe he hates her, too. But why? What has she ever done to him?*

He couldn't answer that one. Perhaps somehow it tied in with the fact that Rose had been engaged to Claude until he died.

Walt's brain was spinning with confusion. He wanted to gallop up to Kenyon's and kill the man with his hands. He wanted the savage satisfaction of a bruising, brutal fight, but he knew that, if he tangled with anyone tonight, he'd be a murderer before he was through.

Chapter Two

He stood there for several moments. In spite of the dying heat of day, he was cold. A chill crept along his spine.

He distrusted his temper and his inclination to go up to Kenyon's now and have it out with the man. Instead, he untied his horse, mounted, and rode aimlessly down the dry bed of the creek.

A pool was drying up, and a dozen trout were in it, trying desperately to stay alive but showing a tendency to turn belly up. They'd all be dead by morning, Walt knew, and this small thing added fuel to his anger. He'd fished the pool as a boy, and had caught many a fighting, gleaming cut-throat trout out of it.

The sun dropped almost reluctantly behind the high mesa to westward, and afterward painted the towering clouds with salmon pink. Walt stared up at the clouds. Why, in God's name, didn't it rain? Moisture was in those clouds, but they always drifted on over and the rain never came.

Yet even now, rain wouldn't solve Ramrod's problems, or even Walt's personal problems. What did men do when something was stolen from them? Walt's expression lightened abruptly. They went to the law. And that's where he would go. Maybe there'd be something Irish McKeogh could do.

He turned out of the creekbed, opened a barbed wire gate, and crossed one of Ramrod's wide fields to the road. His horse was weary and he knew he should have changed before he left. But he hadn't, so he'd have to make the best of it now.

He allowed the animal to walk. Light faded from the sky and the grays of dusk fell across the land. Half a dozen deer, browsing in a field, raised their heads to stare at him, then bounced off out of sight into the locusts that lined the creek.

There was peace in this, the last of the day, and gradually Walt's burning anger began to fade. He was able to look more objectively at the problem facing him.

Kenyon was smart, that was sure. A lone man, fighting a big and powerful ranch, always had a singular advantage, in that sympathy was on his side. Men always sympathized with the underdog. Kenyon was no doubt counting on this, as he was, perhaps, counting on Walt to use force and violence in recovering his water.

For one thing, Kenyon couldn't possibly use four and a half feet of water on his tiny ranch, and he would know Walt knew it. That made Kenyon's move a squeeze play for something else. Something within Walt cautioned him to go slow. Yet with Ramrod drying up, with little or no hay in prospect for wintering their twelve hundred head of cattle, with the old man badgering him and egging him on, with Kenyon himself pressuring, how long would his patience hold out?

He rubbed his stubbled jaw ruefully. Hell, his patience had to hold out. It just wouldn't do to prejudice the court that would eventually hear the water dispute by resorting to violence. Yet, how could he stand by and see Ramrod's hay crop lost, knowing its loss would also mean the loss of cattle or their sacrifice at forced sale during the winter?

Gradually the faint light of dusk faded, and the first of the stars winked out above the towering rims of the plateau.

Walt thought of Rose, knowing he should not have left her as he had, yet knowing also that she would understand.

He left the southern boundary of Ramrod behind, and wound through seven or eight miles of tall, tangy-smelling sagebrush and greasewood, past the winking lights of half a dozen smaller ranches. None of them had much water, but most of them had a little that raised in Wild Horse Creek after it left Ramrod.

At the last small ranch before entering town, the Guilfoile place, Walt's eyes caught movement in the field and he squinted through the pale darkness. There was a horseman out there, apparently pursuing a bunch of horses. They circled the field at a run and came along the fence where it met the road. It was then Rand saw that the horseman was actually a boy.

The boy was almost hysterical. He was crying, and screaming curses at the fleeing horses. Walt shouted— "Tom! Hold it!"—and the boy reined his plunging, lathered horse to a dancing halt.

Walt knew without asking what the trouble was. He even knew to whom the horses belonged. They belonged to Ed Toohey, and ran on the road all year around because Ed figured that was the cheapest way to keep them.

There were those who said Ed taught them to breech fences, but nobody ever proved it. A few extremists claimed Ed always kept a pair of wire cutters in his pocket so he could cut fences, but nobody had ever caught him at it. Every once in a while someone would impound the horses, but Ed always managed to get them away without paying damages, usually by sneaking around in the middle of the night and letting them out.

Tom Guilfoile was about fourteen. He had a shock of straw-colored hair that seemed almost as coarse as straw and a red, liberally freckled face, which was now only a blur in the darkness.

Walt said: "Need some help, Tom?"

"I could sure use it, Walt. Damn them stinkin' bronc's!"

"Where'd they get in?"

The boy gestured with an arm. "Gate down." He was panting as though he had been running.

Walt said: "All right, let's run them out."

He rode down the fence line at a trot until he came to the gate, with Tom pacing him. Something ought to be done about Toohey's horses. Guilfoile's place was one of the smallest on the creek. He couldn't afford to pasture Toohey's horses in his hayfields. Besides that, horses ruined more hay than they ate.

Walt rode through the gate, and the two of them loped across the field toward the bunch, milling against the creek.

Now, seeing two horsemen, they became docile and trotted directly toward the open gate and on through it.

Walt grinned. "They know when they're licked, don't they?"

Tom seemed to have calmed down. But there was quiet anger in him yet. He said: "Someone ought to shoot 'em."

Walt said: "It's not the horses' fault."

"No. Guess not."

Walt went through the gate, and Tom put it up. Leaning on the top wire, he asked: "Walt, when we goin' fishin' again?"

Walt said: "Not enough water to fish. Wait for hunting, this fall." He always took Tom Guilfoile and two or three town boys up to Ramrod's cow camp in the fall to hunt deer. It was one of the year's high points for Walt, who enjoyed the boys' company. He didn't have any of his own yet, and this was next best to taking your own.

Tom mounted, and they sat for a moment in companionable silence, neither having anything to say but both reluctant to leave. The boy had eased the run of temper in Walt and he was more relaxed than he'd been all day.

Tom fidgeted a moment uneasily, then said: "Well, I got to milk. So long, Walt."

" 'Bye, Tom." Walt turned and jogged his weary horse on down the road. Riding without haste, he came at last around a bend and could see the winking, pale lights of the town ahead.

Warbow was an ugly town, yet somehow Walt had never noticed that fact until tonight. Few of its residences had lawns, and those were dry and overgrown with weeds. Boards were missing from the plank walks in enough places to make their use a hazard. Main Street was a sea of dust in summer, a sea of mud in spring and fall, and a mass of frozen ruts in winter.

Along Main, the business buildings were mostly false-fronted, pretending an elegance they did not possess. Without exception, they needed paint. Walt knew that Sonja Zarlengo owned most of them, renting them out and too careful or too careless to spend any of the rentals on upkeep and improvement. He grinned a little at that. Sonja was reputed to be the wealthiest woman in town. Maybe that's how she got that way.

Irish McKeogh's office was down at the end of Main, nestled under the yellow clapboard railroad station. He had bachelor quarters in the rear, having given up his house when Walt married Rose. The jail was a stone building across the street from his office.

Walt saw a light in the rear and so went around that way to knock upon the sagging screen door. He heard Irish bawl: "Come in quick and don't let the damn' flies in."

39

Walt slipped in quickly, but even so a dozen flies of those clustered blackly on the screen entered with him.

Irish McKeogh, the sheriff of Ute County, was sitting beside the stove reading an old newspaper by the inadequate light of a smoking coal-oil lamp on a shelf behind him. The kitchen was stifling hot. Irish looked up, then threw the paper down without bothering to fold it.

He was an abnormally short man, the top of his large head coming only to Walt's chest. His shoulders and hips were like those of a bull and corded with muscle. His biceps were almost the size of Walt's thighs. His hair was graying and curly and worn rather long so that it was like the mane of a lion. He wore a sweeping, cavalry-style mustache that was yellow and streaked with gray. His clothes were dusty and his face unshaven. Sweat stood out on his forehead and stained his shirt. He brushed irritably at a fly that kept trying to land on his nose.

His effort to be agreeable was plainly forced. He stuck out a hand, gripped Walt's, and peered into Walt's face. He said sourly: "Hell's bells, have you an' Rose been fightin', too?"

Walt shook his head. He and Irish had always been close, probably because Irish had raised Rose, his niece, from childhood. Tonight, though, the closeness wasn't there. Walt asked: "What do you mean?"

"Everybody else is fighting. I thought maybe you were, too."

Walt said defensively: "It's going to be me and that god-damn' Kenyon. He's claiming Ramrod's water."

Irish groaned. "Why in hell don't it rain? I've been out the whole damned day. Wes Ordway an' Jess Armstrong got into it up on Rye Creek. Wes is in bed, with one ear and the side of his head sliced off by a shovel. I got Armstrong over in jail. What were they fighting over? A trickle of water out of Rye Creek that wouldn't wet the bottom of a ditch." He drew a breath and scowled at Walt. "Likely I'm goin' to have a murder on my hands before the week's out, too. Dave Lynch came off the mountain last night to find that pimply-faced kid that's been workin' for him sneaking out of the window of his wife's bedroom. He chased the kid afoot through the brush the whole damned night and I chased the pair of 'em all mornin' tryin' to keep 'em apart. God Almighty, do you all have to start fightin' at once?"

Walt glared at him.

Irish growled: "You had supper yet?"

Walt shook his head truculently.

Irish said: "Sit down, then. And cool off."

"In here?"

Irish banged a cup down before him and filled it with thick black coffee from the stove. Walt took a gulp and felt sweat spring from his pores.

Irish asked: "What do you mean, Kenyon's claiming your water?"

"He claims we've given him four and a half feet of water for thirty years, that he's used it and helped maintain the ditch. Claims that gives him a right to it. Bryce is backing him up."

"Hell, he can't use four and a half feet."

"I know he can't."

Irish grinned suddenly. "I'd like to have heard what Jake had to say."

Walt said: "It wasn't funny."

"No. It wouldn't be . . . to you." The sheriff gave him a searching look, then turned to the stove. He filled the two plates from the skillets and then set them, empty, in the sink. He took the lamp from the shelf and put it between them. A mothmiller, aroused from some cranny by the changing rays of light, flitted wildly around the glass chimney for a moment, bumping against it, then found the opening and plopped inside. The flames seared him and he fell against the wick, slowly frying and kicking his last.

Irish, ever a man to find a parallel, said: "See that? That's what everybody in the whole damned country is actin' like. Crazy. What is it about heat and drought that makes people act that way? Kenyon don't need your water. So why'd he take it?"

Walt shrugged. The heat of the room seemed to be closing in on him. At last he said: "I don't know what's eating Kenyon. But I expect the rest of them are scared. They've spent years building up their herds. If they can't make hay this year, they'll have to sell, and it'll be at a give-away price because the situation's no better other places than it is right here. Everybody'll be selling and no one buying. Ramrod's in the same fix. We've got twelve hundred cattle, and, if we don't get that water back, we won't be able to feed two hundred through the winter. What I want to know is . . . what are you going to do about it?"

Irish stared at him over the smoking lamp of the chimney. He seemed not to notice the smoke. At last he said: "Walt, you knew damned well when you came here that there was nothing I could do. Kenyon's made a claim to your water. He's got the water and the claim sounds legal. With Bryce backing him up, it's a matter for the courts, not the sheriff's office. What the hell did you give him water for, anyway? You know it's supposed to go back in the creek when you're through with it."

Walt's eyes had suddenly grown hard. "I'm not going to the courts, Irish. I need that water now, not next summer, after the court's fooled around with it for a year. That's

Ramrod water, and, by God, I'm going to have it. Just because we've always been generous with Kenyon. . . ."

Irish pushed the lamp aside. His cold gray eyes bored straight into Walt's. His words were clipped and harsh. "I like you, Walt. You're married to Rose and that makes you part of my own family. But step outside the law and you'll get the same treatment from me that I'd give any lawbreaker. Use your head, boy. This is exactly what Kenyon's playing for. He wants you to lose your temper. He's crowdin' you. Take that water back and you'll find an injunction slapped against you. Take it back after that and you're in real trouble . . . prison trouble."

Anger crawled unpleasantly in the back of Walt's mind. He could feel its steady growth, and he looked across the table at Irish McKeogh as though he were a stranger. He heard his own words coming unbidden from his mouth: "You sound as if you were in cahoots with him."

Irish stood up abruptly and violently. His chair tipped over and fell behind him. His voice was menacing. "Watch your talk, Walt! Watch your talk!"

Walt got up slowly. Anger was now a steady, driving force in the back of his mind. He said softly: "You want to try and make me watch my talk, Irish?"

For a moment they stood there, glaring at each other. In Walt was a deep, overpowering sense of injustice. Something had been taken from him that was rightfully his. To compound the injustice, here was the sheriff telling him there was nothing to do about it.

But there was more to it than that, and Walt recognized it even though he was unable to understand it. It was as though he were being pushed into the things he did against his will. He didn't want to fight with Irish McKeogh, nor did he feel that Irish was dishonest.

Irish said exasperatedly: "For God's sake, Walt, this ain't like you, or me, either. What's the matter with us? Go on down to Sonja's place and get yourself a drink. Then, if you feel like talking, come back."

Walt wanted to stick out his hand, but he didn't. He couldn't right now. He growled—"Thanks for the supper."—turned, and walked out, banging the screen door behind him.

He had the oddest feeling that he ought to take Rose and leave the country tonight, while there was still time. Something was building up here in the valley, something ugly and beyond understanding.

He shook his head impatiently. He untied his horse, but did not mount. Instead, he stood hesitating, disliking himself and the unreasoning temper that had made him fight with Irish, who he sincerely liked.

At last, impulsively and quickly, he left the horse and strode back across the yard. He banged into the house, colliding with Irish, who still stood squarely in the door.

He backed off, and suddenly began to laugh. When he could talk, he choked out the words: "Irish, I'm sorry."

Irish, surprised, began to chuckle. He said: "It's all right, Walt. Forget it. Now go on and get your drink."

Walt turned, feeling foolish, but a lot better than he had a few moments before. He mounted, and grinned to himself in the darkness. Then he rode on uptown toward Sonja Zarlengo's place. Maybe Irish was right. Maybe what he needed was a drink—a drink and a good night's sleep.

Chapter Three

There were two saloons in Warbow. Both were owned by Sonja Zarlengo, but only one was called Sonja's Place. The other was known as the Horse Head, although in pronunciation the name invariably came out Whore's Head.

Sonja's Place pretended elegance, having a carved oak back-bar she'd bought in some fading gold camp and, above it, the naked, reclining figure of a voluptuous woman, smiling invitingly at all who stood at the bar. It was a trick of the painting that the woman seemed to be looking directly at each man, no matter where he happened to be standing. The painting bore a certain resemblance to Sonja herself, which gave rise to considerable ribald speculation as to how the painter was able to keep his mind on painting with Sonja looking at him like that.

Other than the back-bar and the painting, however, there was little about Sonja's Place that was extraordinary. The bar was worn and scarred, particularly down near the brass rail where spurs had gouged and left their marks. The rest of the room was filled with the usual complement of round tables surrounded by rickety chairs. Most nights there'd be two or three poker games going, usually for small stakes. Nickel ante—two-bit limit. Tonight, because of the heat, the swinging doors were held open by screen door hooks on the inside walls. Smoke and the sour odor of spilled whiskey greeted Walt as he stepped inside.

There were two or three men at the bar, all of whom Walt knew. Over against the wall a couple of strange kids about eighteen or nineteen were playing poker with a couple of local kids. The faces of all four were oddly intent, and none of them looked up as Walt entered.

Walt stepped over to the bar, fumbling in the pocket of his jeans for a coin. He came up with a half dollar and laid it on the bar. Will Harsh, the bartender, put a hand on the beer tap and slid a glass under it. Before he could fill the glass, Walt said: "Make it whiskey, Will."

Harsh looked surprised. Walt never drank whiskey in summer, particularly on nights as hot as this one. Harsh shrugged and slid bottle and glass expertly down the bar to Walt. Harsh had seen the thin edge of temper in Walt.

Walt poured himself a drink, tossed it off, and, wiping his mouth with the back of his hand, turned his attention to the other three at the bar. One was John Massey, round and dark-haired and shrewd of eye. He looked at Walt and winked. "Some days nothin' goes right, Walt. Just come off the mountain?"

Walt nodded. He said: "Hoof rot, poison weeds, crew fightin' among themselves. Down here, it's water." He shook his head disgustedly and poured another drink. The first was a comfortable, warm feeling in his stomach already.

Hamp Richards, a rodent-faced small man with a place on Rye Creek, asked: "Hear about Ordway an' Armstrong? Ordway got himself earmarked with a shovel. Armstrong got a free room in McKeogh's hotel."

Walt nodded. "I heard."

Lew Purdy, the gigantic, mild-mannered blacksmith, rumbled in his gentle way: "Violence solves none of mankind's problems. It only makes them worse."

Hamp cackled. "Tell Dave Lynch that, Lew. Tell Dave an unviolent way of handling a hired man you catch leaving your wife's bedroom carrying his pants." He cackled again, watching Walt for reaction. Walt grinned, but the grin was forced.

He liked Lew Purdy, because you couldn't help liking the big, simple man. He wondered sometimes if Lew was quite as simple as he seemed. A lot of Lew's talk made sense. He liked John Massey, too. Massey ran the feed store, and, although he was shrewd, he never tried to take advantage of shortages in fixing his feed prices. But Walt had never cared for Hamp Richards. Maybe Hamp was too much like old Jake. You could never tell what direction his sly remarks were pointing.

Hamp had been talking. Walt missed the first part of what he had said, but caught the last: ". . . man hadn't ought to come home unexpected unless he's damn' sure of his wife. And who is?"

Walt was irritated with himself for remembering the glimpse he'd caught this afternoon of a brown horse's rump disappearing into the locusts that fringed the creek, and for remembering Jake's insinuations. He shook his head angrily.

Hamp went on babbling, telling a story of someone over in the Salt Wash country who'd come home unexpectedly and had solved the problem in a comical and unorthodox way. Walt chuckled, but his chuckle died as he realized Hamp had been watching him covertly throughout the story. Again he felt his anger stir. What the hell was Hamp getting at? Was there something sly and special behind his choice of a subject tonight? He scowled at Hamp and poured himself another drink.

John Massey said bluntly: "Shut up, Hamp. Your smoking-car humor gets old fast." Massey turned to Walt. "I hear there's some last year's hay to be had down near Douglas. It'll cost like hell to get it here, maybe twenty-five dollars a ton, but it's better than a snow bank. You want me to check into it?"

Walt nodded wearily. You couldn't feed twenty-five dollar hay to cattle that sold for three cents a pound, but you couldn't let them starve, either. He was warmed by the look in Massey's eyes, for it was a look of genuine liking and sympathy for the problems that faced him. Massey knew Jake. He knew the way Jake always threw Claude at Walt. He knew Walt was carrying the whole load at Ramrod and getting nothing but trouble from Jake in return.

Massey said: "This is going to be a bad year. When people start having trouble, they start looking around for a goat."

Lew Purdy nodded ponderously as though Massey had uttered something of profound wisdom. Walt heard a horse trotting down the street outside and tossed off his third drink. A horse at the saloon rail nickered and the hoof beat stopped. Walt glanced around curiously.

Light fell through the door and dimly illuminated the plank walk outside and part of the dusty street. Walt saw the unmistakable form of Nick Kenyon leave the tie rail and step toward the door.

Something seemed to draw up and tighten in Walt's mind. He could feel the muscles of his body grow tense. He glared at Kenyon, but the big man did not look at him, a circumstance that only further tended to infuriate Walt. Kenyon knew he was here, damn him. He certainly hadn't missed seeing Walt's horse. He'd tied right beside him.

Kenyon was big, perhaps twenty pounds heavier than Walt's own hundred and seventy-five. He was thirty-five, but his face looked ten years younger than that, due perhaps to its full roundness. The fleshiness ended there. Kenyon's body was as lean and hard as Walt's own.

Even had Walt not been prejudiced against Kenyon because of the man's repeated water thefts, he would not have liked him, for there was something false about Kenyon's brash, ready smile, the smile which seemed to captivate women so. Beneath the smile, Walt decided, Kenyon was a brooding and unpredictably dangerous man. He was carrying a grudge against the world.

He glared hard at Kenyon, trying now to make the man look at him. Kenyon shoved his hat back to reveal a thinning crop of fine yellow hair through which his scalp showed, pink as his flushed and sweating face.

Kenyon grinned at the three that stood there together down near the end of the bar. He walked to the bar between Walt and the three. He ordered a beer from Harsh and, as Harsh drew it, turned a quick glance toward Walt.

What Walt had been prepared for, he didn't know. Humility, perhaps, or sheepishness. Maybe even brashness that dared Walt to recover the water Kenyon had patently stolen. But certainly he wasn't prepared for what he saw— the most virulent, venomous hatred he had ever seen in the eyes of a man. For an instant it was like a dash of cold water, stunning him, and then it made him mad.

His shoulders bunched and he pushed back away from the bar. Kenyon seized the beer glass Harsh shoved at him and flung the contents into Walt's face. Walt swung a hard, bony fist.

It was so spontaneous and sudden that for a moment the other occupants of Sonja's Place stared in bewilderment. Then they backed hastily out of the way.

Kenyon pedaled halfway across the room, driven back by the impetus of Walt's fist against his jaw. The sound of it seemed to hang in the room, a crisp, solid sound of bone against bone, cushioned only by a thin layer of flesh.

Walt crouched and charged, his booted feet skidding a

little with the driving force of his legs. He put his head down and struck Kenyon with it exactly in Kenyon's middle just as he was beginning to get his balance again. Kenyon released a gigantic *whoof*. Off balance, he jackknifed and sat down hard with an impact that shook the building and rattled the bottles on the back-bar. His hands went up, caught Walt's neck, and yanked him down, too. Walt's momentum kept him going and he rolled head over heels out the door and into the street.

By the time he had gained his feet, Kenyon was coming. Walt braced himself, ducked, and swung a hard right at Kenyon's middle. Kenyon's boot, rising to kick, caught Walt's wrist with enough force to lift his arm and fist into the air over his head. Pain shot through the arm clear to Walt's shoulder. Mist swam before his eyes.

Kenyon, off balance from the kick, recovered quickly and raised a knee toward Walt's groin that would have ended the fight. Walt doubled and caught the knee against his chest. Its force was frightening and all but knocked the wind out of him, but he caught Kenyon's leg, straightened, and yanked backward, using his weight to dump Kenyon.

Kenyon fell, and Walt lunged at him, landing with both knees in Kenyon's middle. Again that *whoof*, but Kenyon seemed in no way weakened. His right arm came flashing up, and the elbow caught Walt in the throat. He felt as though a giant hand had closed his windpipe. He choked, and gagged, and rolled from atop Kenyon, trying with desperation to get his breath.

As he rolled, a corner of his eye saw Harsh and the others and the four kids who had been playing poker clustered in the saloon doorway.

Kenyon was after Walt like a cat, sensing that this was the time for the kill. He aimed a boot at Walt's head. It landed, but Walt was still rolling away, and much of the kick's force was lost.

Walt was still trying to suck air into his starving lungs. He felt as he had one time when he'd fallen into the raging spring run-off in Wild Horse Creek. There wasn't any air coming into his lungs.

Something hard slammed into his leg, and he realized suddenly that he had rolled beneath one of the horses tied at the rail. The animal was spooked and frightened and was trying to kick him out from beneath it. The horse's shod hoofs constituted an even deadlier threat than Kenyon's fists. He came to hands and knees and lunged away from the horse, meeting Kenyon in an unplanned, awkward collision that stopped them both.

There was no science in this, and little skill. It was a battle of savages, who knew no rule but to destroy. Walt put his head against Kenyon's chest and pumped half a dozen vicious blows into the big man's mid-section. Kenyon, grunting, countered by bringing his two clasped hands down like a club against Walt's neck.

Walt's throat was opening now and breath made a high, whistling sound as it passed back and forth into and out of his lungs. The blow on his neck drove him down into the dirt of the street. Kenyon kicked and his boot heel was like a club striking the top of Walt's head.

Gray mists swirled before Walt's eyes. That should have finished him, but he neither admitted it nor even knew it. Kenyon drew back his foot for another kick, but Walt, scrambling along the ground on elbows and knees, caught the booted foot in both hands and jerked.

He both avoided the kick and dumped Kenyon neatly to the ground. He crawled up Kenyon's body like a squirrel climbs a tree, straddled him, and began to slash with fists and elbows at Kenyon's bleeding face.

Dust rose around them in a cloud. The horses at the rail turned their heads, ears laid back, eyes rolling. They crowded each other to get away from the thrashing bodies on the ground, but every now and then one would kick out as a man might kick at a pair of fighting dogs who rolled against his legs.

Kenyon's hands, failing in their try for Walt's eyes, reached back for purchase and encountered a loose plank in the boardwalk. He tore it loose. He brought it straight over his head, but Walt dodged aside and caught it on his shoulder.

He grabbed the board, lunged to his feet, and tore it from Kenyon's grasp. He used it like a bat and shattered it on the side of Kenyon's head. Kenyon crawled to retrieve a broken end of it, and Walt booted him hard on his narrow, muscled rump. Off balance, Kenyon was driven forward, directly under the fidgeting hoofs of the frightened horses.

They plunged and whinnied shrilly, and one of them reared, breaking the reins looped around the rail. The horse galloped away down the street, but nobody moved to follow.

Kenyon tried to get up, and his back bumped the belly of the horse directly above him. The horse humped and kicked savagely, but his hoofs were unable to reach the man.

Standing there, hunched a little against the pain in his chest and throat, breathing gustily, Walt heard Sonja Zarlengo's excited, angry voice as she sought to push through the doorway filled with gaping spectators.

He brushed blood from his mouth and took a staggering step toward Kenyon, who was now up between two of the horses, trying to work his way toward the rail and duck under it.

Kenyon's hand must have encountered the stock of

someone's rifle protruding from a saddle boot, for he stopped and yanked it clear. He levered it, laid it across the neck of the horse nearest Walt, and pulled the trigger. The gun made an empty *click*.

For some reason, this attempt to kill him infuriated Walt more than anything that had gone before. He charged toward Kenyon, staggering a little but not realizing it. Kenyon ducked under the tie rail, still holding the rifle, and Walt vaulted it just as Kenyon swung the rifle.

His legs struck the swinging rifle and Kenyon at the same time, and the pair piled up together on the sidewalk, after rolling and thrashing thunderously like two boys scrapping in a schoolyard. Only this was deadly now, and the will to kill was in them both.

Sonja Zarlengo screamed: "Stop it! Harsh, stop them!" When no one paid her any mind, she seized big Lew Purdy by a bronzed and corded arm. "Stop them, Lew! Stop them before they kill each other!"

Lew shuffled toward the pair uncertainly. He stopped halfway to them and looked back at Sonya pleadingly, but she was adamant. "Go on, Lew. Stop them!"

Lew came on, ponderously unhurried and with no enthusiasm for interference, much as he disliked violence.

Kenyon was still clinging desperately to the rifle, trying to use it as a club and permanently failing for he could not get room to swing. Walt grabbed two fistfuls of his hair and began to bang his head against the plank walk. It made a steady thudding sound, and, although none of the separate impacts was severe enough to knock Kenyon out, the combined force of all of them apparently was. Slowly his eyes began to glaze. Slowly the savage expression of hatred on his face began to relax. His lips grew slack and his eyes grew blank.

Walt's vision was a fuzzy, red haze. He neither saw nor

felt Kenyon's body grow limp, and continued to thump the unconscious man's head against the boardwalk. In his throat was a low growl that had no words.

Big Lew Purdy reached down almost reluctantly and grasped a handful of his shirt. Lew lifted him up the way you'd lift a dog out of a fight. He kept saying in his gentle, apologetic voice: "You quit it now, Walt. You ain't aimin' to kill him, are you? You quit it now an' cool off. Tomorrow you'll be glad you did."

Walt swung at him, but the blow missed.

Lew said softly: "Walt, you don't want to hit me. You're just mad."

The softness of the big man's voice had its soothing effect on Walt. He shook his head. "All right, Lew. All right."

Lew released him. Walt staggered to the edge of the walk and sat down. He dropped his head between his knees and sat there, breathing hoarsely and shallowly because of the pain in his throat and chest.

How long he sat there he didn't know. It must have been a long, long time. Dimly he heard voices around him. Then they were gone.

An oddly pleasant smell made him raise his head. The street was deserted, save for himself and Sonja Zarlengo, who sat beside him. The smell was Sonja's perfume. Walt looked at her blankly.

She said: "You can't go home that way, Walt. Come in and wash up. I'll find you a clean shirt. By that time, maybe you'll be in shape to ride."

He could feel the softness and warmth of her hands as she helped him rise. For a moment he couldn't remember who he had fought or what the fight was about. He followed her blindly, half unconscious, into the deserted saloon in which a single coal-oil lamp burned.

Chapter Four

Walt had never been upstairs to Sonja's quarters, although there had been times when he'd thought about it. He guessed every man in Warbow had thought about it, at least every man young enough to feel desire. Sonja was a damned beautiful woman.

Kenyon saw her occasionally, and the town, knowing she had once been his father's wife, made sly, suggestive remarks about his visits. There were some who said Irish McKeogh visited her, too, but Walt was inclined to doubt it. Sonja may have had a love life, but, if she did, it was her own secret.

She led him through the dim saloon to a door at the rear. It opened into a dark hallway. Walt stumbled, and she reached around and found his hand with her own. Thereafter she led him, like a small boy, up the steep stairs.

He didn't know what he expected exactly—perhaps a fluffy apartment of bright silks and feathers and naked pink kewpie dolls, like one he had seen over in Denver that belonged to one of Mattie Silks's girls. Head hanging wearily, he waited just inside the door for Sonja to strike a match.

She did, and lighted a lamp, and he saw for the first time what her home looked like. There was a deep-piled Oriental rug on the floor. Against one wall was a period sofa upholstered in gold brocade. Green velvet drapes hung at the windows, and in front of them was an onyx-topped table with a marble statuette on it. The chairs were comfortable and each had its crocheted doilies on arms and back. Walt caught a glimpse of Sonya's bedroom through a partly open door, and, although he didn't see much, he saw the bed with its yellow satin spread. It was a calmly furnished and thoroughly comfortable apartment. Sonja might be thrifty about repairs to her buildings, but she'd apparently spared no expense here. Walt looked at her with new respect.

She said with slight impatience: "Sit down, Walt, before you fall down. I'll get water and soap."

He looked down at his dusty, blood-spattered jeans, started to brush them off, and changed his mind. He crossed the room to a straight-backed chair and straddled it gingerly, leaning his arms on its back.

She returned in a moment with pitcher and basin and towel. She knelt before him, saying: "Now let me do this. There are some nasty cuts on your face."

He flushed with embarrassment, but did not protest. Gently she dabbed at his face and, when it was clean, blotted it with the towel. She held the pan for him while he washed his skinned and bloody hands, then carried the pan away. "Take off your shirt."

Walt stood up, feeling refreshed. He took off his torn shirt, looked at it, then wadded it up in his hands. His chest was hairy and corded with muscles that tightened with each small movement. There were angry red blotches where Kenyon's fists had landed, and one bleeding, scratched place where apparently one of the horses had kicked him.

Sonja returned with a white shirt and modestly averted her glance from his naked chest as she handed it to him. He put it on quickly, wondering at this modesty in her. He frowned slightly, knowing that, if it was feigned, she was being coquettish. And if she was, she was interested in him. He grinned at himself. How a man's thoughts did go on. Hell, he was married, and happily married, too.

He buttoned the shirt, and she looked at his face, her own slightly pink. "What was the fight about, Walt?"

He had to smile. "About? Hell, neither one of us said a word."

For a moment she stood looking at him, perplexed, as though trying to decide if he were ribbing her. She was tall for a woman and was, perhaps, thirty-five. She was attractive, able to stir a man ten years her junior in spite of weariness and hurt and the fact that he loved his wife at home.

Her body was voluptuous, and, if the portrait over the bar was any guide, made to the proportions of a Venus. Her skin was clear and white, touched with freckles across her nose. Her mouth was too large for perfection, but the cumulative effect of her features surpassed mere beauty.

Walt wondered fleetingly at the pressures that had shaped her life. Nobody knew much about her, only that she had been married briefly to Olaf Kenyon before he died, and that after his death she had disappeared only to return several years later under her maiden name and with a substantial bank account. Looking at her, Walt couldn't believe the town's gossip that she was having an affair with Kenyon, her former husband's son. She didn't seem the type for that.

She said, her voice throaty and pleasant: "Walt, you didn't fight just for the joy of fighting. You're not that kind of man. There had to be a reason."

He said: "There was. Kenyon has seized Ramrod's water and is laying claim to it. Irish says we'll have to disprove it in court, but I'm not satisfied that there isn't another way."

She was incredulous. "Seized your water? How can he do that? And why would he want to? You've always given him water when he needed it. I can vouch for that."

Walt grinned ruefully. "That's the rub. We're not supposed to give water to anyone. If we'd been less generous all these years, we wouldn't be in the fix we're in."

He was wondering suddenly why Jake had given water to the Kenyons and probing his memory for the answer. Certainly it hadn't been because he liked Olaf Kenyon, Nick's father. Walt could remember how bitter Jake became whenever Olaf Kenyon's name was mentioned to him.

Still, Walt had only been ten years old at the time Kenyon died. He and Jake might have been friends once. Their hostility might have come later. Maybe that was it. Perhaps Jake and Olaf had been good friends. Maybe Jake had begun giving him water out of friendship or from obligation. Certainly Jake wasn't naturally generous. Quite the contrary, he was miserly and tight, and, if Walt's memory served, always had been.

Suddenly Walt started inwardly with surprise. Why the hell hadn't it occurred to him before? Sonja Zarlengo had been Olaf Kenyon's wife, although she was actually no older than Olaf's son. Many things dated back exactly fifteen years: Olaf's death, Jake's stroke, and Sonja's departure.

Interest stirred in Walt's thoughts. Could there be some connection? Could Jake have been in love with Sonja? Couldn't there have been a quarrel over her between Olaf and Jake, resulting in Olaf's death and Jake's paralysis?

He said, mildly startling Sonja as much by the way he was looking at her as by what he said: "Kids are awful damned blind, aren't they, Sonja?"

She smiled uncertainly. "What is that supposed to mean? We were talking about water."

He said: "Never mind. I've got to get home."

There was an odd shyness in her. "I suppose you should. People talk about me enough as it is."

Excitement stirred in Walt, for he recognized in her

remark a reluctance to see him go. She wanted him to stay. But there was a kind of defenselessness about her that did not escape his notice.

He started to reach for her and changed his mind. If Jake had been in love with her, there would be something indecent about Walt's making love to her. Besides, he was suddenly seeing Rose in his thoughts and wanting nothing so much as to be at home where Rose was.

Fright had showed briefly in Sonja's eyes as he moved toward her. It subsided when he changed his mind, to be replaced by an odd mixture of relief and some disappointment.

He said, completely surprised by Sonja now: "Thanks for all you've done, Sonja. I feel a lot better than I did."

"You're all right to ride?"

He grinned. "Sure."

She walked with him to the door. "How's your father, Walt?"

"All right. Ornery as ever. Sometimes I wonder what eats on him."

Her expression was strange. Suddenly, inexplicably, she reached up and kissed him on the cheek. "Go on home now, Walt. And no more fighting, hear?"

"All right." He followed her down the stairs and through the scattered tables to the outside door, frowning with bewilderment. His horse was the only one there at the rail.

Sonja stood in the saloon doorway until he had mounted. Then she closed the inside doors and he heard a padlock slipped into a hasp on the inside.

He rode out of town, every muscle aching with the movements of the horse. For a few moments he puzzled over Sonja's strange behavior. For a while there, she had seemed like a woman who wanted to be loved. But at the last she had treated him more as a mother would. He shook his head in complete bewilderment.

He thought of Kenyon, realizing that the fight had solved nothing. Kenyon still had the water, and, however doubtful his claim to it, Walt was deprived of it for the duration of the irrigation season. That hatred he'd seen in Kenyon's eyes was what puzzled him. Kenyon had courted Rose and lost her. But was that enough reason for such undiluted hatred? Walt doubted it.

He had never liked Kenyon, but had never disliked him, either. He certainly had never done anything to hurt the man, so that couldn't be it. But if Kenyon's hatred had been terrible before, it would now be doubly so. Walt had beaten him, and a beating would be a hard thing for Kenyon to take.

He shook his aching head impatiently. His throat was still sore from Kenyon's blow, and he swallowed frequently. Tomorrow he'd have to ride into town and see Sidney Bryce, the water commissioner. He'd exhaust all legal means of recovering his irrigation water.

He knew one thing. He wasn't going to stand by and let Kenyon have water he didn't need at Ramrod's expense. Walt had notes to meet this winter. Loss of the hay crop could mean a serious financial loss, one from which Ramrod might not recover. If Bryce and McKeogh wouldn't help, then Walt would have no choice but to take back the water by force.

It was nearly two when he rode into the yard at Ramrod. The windows were dark, with a single exception—his own bedroom.

His hands shook as he unsaddled his horse. He ran across the yard to the house, his hurts eased by the stimulation of excitement. He entered the house quietly. He didn't want Jake butting in.

She waited at the top of the stairs. She wore a thin cotton nightgown with lace at the throat. The light from the bedroom door behind her outlined every curve of her delicate figure through the transparent gown. Her hair was down, lustrous and beautiful as though she had been brushing it for hours. Her voice was worried, and a little timid. "Walt? Where have you been?"

"Town. I wanted to see Irish."

He reached the top of the stairs and gathered her into his arms. She was warm against him. Her arms went around his neck eagerly and her face buried itself in his chest.

She was like a doll, and he picked her up and carried her into the bedroom. He kicked the door shut behind him, carried her over, and laid her down on the bed. He started to kiss her, but she pushed him away, her eyes widening. "Walt, what happened?"

He grinned sheepishly, stood up, and removed his shirt. "Had a fight with Kenyon."

"Over the water?"

He nodded. He wadded up the shirt and tossed it in a corner, wondering guiltily if she'd recognized it as being different from the one he'd had on earlier—or if she'd place its origin—but how could she? Reassured, he sat down on the edge of the bed and pulled off his boots.

"Couldn't Irish do anything for you?"

"Couldn't, or wouldn't."

"Walt, what do you mean?"

"Nothing. I guess I meant he couldn't. Kenyon's got Bryce behind him."

She touched the bruises on his chest with her soft, gentle hands. "You poor darling."

Hunger leaped in Walt. He got up and crossed the room. He blew out the lamp and felt his way back to her. The moon came shining through the window, illuminating her upper body and part of her face.

He chuckled. "To hell with Kenyon. He's worse off right now than I am. He hasn't got you."

He lay down beside her and crushed her to him, and for a little while there was nothing in the world for him but the fierce ecstasy of assuaging hunger and expressing love.

But later, when she lay sleeping peacefully beside him with the moonlight soft on her relaxed and faintly smiling face, he thought of his own words and wondered at them. "He's worse off right now than I am. He hasn't got you."

He remembered the shock he'd felt, seeing such terrible hatred on Kenyon's face. He remembered the way Kenyon had of looking at Rose.

Chapter Five

Walt slept very little during the night. His mind was too busy. It seemed incredible that Kenyon could have stolen the water just out of jealousy, and yet what else could he think? Kenyon couldn't possibly use that much water, and it was doubtful if the court which eventually heard the dispute would award him that much. Walt suspected the court would give Kenyon something, but it wouldn't be over a foot for a place the size of Kenyon's. He was convinced that Kenyon's grab was not a squeeze play for money. If it had been, Kenyon would have offered some kind of proposition.

The sky outside the window of the room turned gray with dawn. Walt swung his feet over the edge of the bed and sat up. Rose stirred sleepily, then opened her eyes and looked at him.

He crossed the room to the bureau and found a clean shirt and a clean pair of jeans. He put them on, then sat down again on the edge of the bed to pull on his boots.

Rose asked, awake now: "What are you going to do?"

"Go into Warbow and see Bryce."

"What if he tells you there's nothing you can do?"

His eyes hardened. "I don't know. I'll cross that bridge when I come to it." But he had already crossed it, and Rose knew he had. Her face grew still.

He looked at her and said: "Kenyon's still in love with you. Did you know that?"

She flushed darkly. Walt stifled an unreasoning anger that rose instantly in his mind. She had known it.

He said: "I've never in my life seen more hatred in a man's eyes than I saw in Kenyon's last night."

Rose bounded out of bed and put on a pink satin wrap. She looked at Walt, her eyes sparkling dangerously. "If you're trying to say something, Walt, say it."

He said: "All right, I will. It seems mighty funny to me that Kenyon should suddenly be jealous of me unless he's been seeing you. Has he?"

Her arm swung, and her small hand collided sharply with the side of Walt's face.

His eyes blazed, and then the fire died. He said: "Maybe I deserved that. Maybe not. What was Kenyon doing here yesterday afternoon?"

Her face flushed, whether from anger or guilt, he couldn't tell. She said: "He's been pestering me just as he did before Claude and I became engaged. He finds all kinds of excuses for coming here, and some of his reasons are pretty thin. But, Walt, that's not my fault. I've never done anything to encourage him."

For a moment they stood there glaring at each other. Within himself, Walt could feel the rise of yesterday's unreasoning anger. He didn't really doubt Rose. Yet if he didn't, why this stubborn unwillingness to apologize for his suspicions?

The words came hard to his throat: "Honey, I'm sorry."

She smiled stiffly, her eyes holding a residue of anger. "So am I, Walt. Come on, now, I'll get you some breakfast."

He followed her down the stairs. What closeness had been between them last night was gone. Walt thought unwillingly of the glimpse he'd caught yesterday of Kenyon's horse disappearing into the locusts. He thought of Dave Lynch chasing his hired hand. He cursed himself inwardly, but he couldn't stop his thoughts. He couldn't help going back, remembering that Rose had been engaged to Claude until Claude had frozen to death in November. He couldn't help wondering if he had not been second choice, a kind of consolation prize. Maybe that was what had nagged him all these months. Lord knew, Jake drummed it into him often enough that he wasn't half the man Claude had been.

He sat at the kitchen table watching her, hating himself for his doubting thoughts. He heard the iron tires of Jake's wheelchair, and turned his head toward the door.

Jake rolled through it, scowling. He stared at Walt for a moment, then said sarcastically: "You're a hell of a sorry lookin' mess. Who'd you tangle with?"

"Kenyon."

Jake chuckled humorlessly. "I suppose he wiped up the saloon with you."

Walt said: "He didn't."

"You mean you whipped him?"

Walt nodded. Jake opened his mouth to say something, but Walt cut him short: "You started the trouble we're in by giving Olaf Kenyon water thirty years ago. Why? I never knew you to give anything away in your whole damned life. Why'd you give Olaf water? What was in it for you?"

Jake's eyes narrowed. "We were friends. I talked him into coming here. The water was all taken, so I gave him part of ours."

Walt had the obscure feeling that he had Jake on the defensive, and it puzzled him. He was determined not to let his advantage slip away, so he said: "You and Olaf fought fifteen years ago, didn't you? What was the fight about?"

He had expected anger in his father at that question, but he had certainly not expected the reaction he got. Jake's face went white, then became congested with blood. The old man's chest labored to supply air to his lungs. His breath came in short gasps. His body stiffened. His eyes looked at Walt with an expression of intense pain.

Rose cried: "Walt! He's having another stroke!"

Walt leaped around the table and snatched his father's frail body from the wheelchair, startled at its lack of substance. He carried the old man back to his bedroom and laid him on the bed. Rose pushed Walt aside and started to loosen old Jake's collar.

But Jake struggled up to a sitting position. He pushed her away peevishly. "Go on. Let me alone."

Walt's breath sighed out with relief. The old man lifted his paralyzed legs with his hands in the peculiarly awkward way he had, and swung them over the side of the bed. He said: "Go get my wheelchair."

Rose went to get it, throwing a cautioning glance over her shoulder at Walt. It wasn't needed. Walt had no intention of bringing up the subject of Jake's fight with Olaf again.

When Rose came back, she shoved the chair close to the bed, and Jake eased himself into it, using only his hands. You had to hand it to him, Walt thought. He was self-sufficient and required a minimum amount of care for an invalid. There was surprising strength in his frail-looking arms. He dressed and undressed himself, got in and out of the wheelchair, and even rolled himself to the outhouse behind the house.

Now he said, without looking either at Walt or Rose: "I want my breakfast." Walt thought he was almost like a small boy who had a secret he wanted to keep, and was deliberately steering the conversation away from anything that might jeopardize it.

Walt said: "I'll be going."

"You haven't had breakfast," Rose said.

"I'll get something in town."

He looked at her, the things they wished to say remaining unsaid. Then he turned and went out the front door, grabbing up his hat as he went.

The sun was just rising above the towering plateau, throwing its hot, brassy rays into the valley. Already it was hot and Walt began to sweat as he roped a horse out of the corral and saddled.

Old Mac, who batched in the bunkhouse while the crew was on top of the mountain, came to the door. Walt rode to him and sat looking down. He said: "Mac, I'll have your water back before tomorrow. Take it easy today."

Mac's face was covered with graying whiskers. His skin was like antique leather from being so much in the sun. He wore a pair of farmer's overalls and an undershirt. His eyes were watery and beginning to look vague. He said: "You be careful, son. Gettin' that there water back is goin' to be like stealin' honey from a wild beehive. You could git stung."

Walt grinned. "I'll be careful."

"Don't you be wonderin' what Claude would have done. Claude wouldn't've done a bit better than you're doin'. Hear?"

Walt said gratefully: "Sure, Mac. Sure."

He rode out, wondering what had happened to Kenyon last night. Had the man gotten up and gone home under his own power? Or had Massey and the others carried him to the hotel and put him to bed?

Walt didn't feel good. The direct, bright rays of the sun had started his head to aching. The scene with Jake and the disagreement with Rose had upset him. He was hungry, and his bruised body now began to ache again from the motion of the horse. He realized that he was in a poor frame of mind to be going to see Bryce. He'd probably quarrel with the man. An edge of truculence touched his thoughts. After all, wasn't Bryce teamed up in an inexcusable water steal with Kenyon?

He puzzled about that for a moment. What was there about this heat and drought that so revived old hatreds? Walt knew Bryce had been crowded off his range by Ramrod years ago, and he knew Bryce hated Jake for it. But why had he waited until now to work out his hatred?

The horse was fresh, so he let the animal gallop until he tired and dropped back into a trot of his own accord. The miles flowed behind, but Walt's temper did not improve. There was something exceedingly depressing about mile after mile of scorched fields. He passed several men he knew working small streams of water in their fields but none of them waved in their usual friendly way. They just tipped back their hats and stared, unmoving and stiffly hostile, until he had gone on past.

He thought angrily each time—*What the hell's the matter with you?*—and after a while stopped raising his arm to wave. Had they heard about his fight with Kenyon? Did they sympathize with the man? Probably that was it. Right or wrong, Kenyon was a small landowner like themselves. It struck a chord of sympathy within each of them to see Kenyon fighting the Rands, and the sympathy had been increased by the beating Rand had given Kenyon last night.

Once again, Walt had the inexplicable feeling that something ugly was growing here in this valley where he'd lived out his life. So far, it had only been a feeling, yet today there were tangible signs of it in the faces of everyone he met. He could imagine how Hamp Richards had spent the night. Hamp had probably stopped at every ranch on both Wild Horse and Rye Creeks.

These men who looked so coldly at him this morning

were, Walt decided, angered as he was angered at heat and drought and helplessness. They needed something tangible upon which to vent their rage. Kenyon, by boldly and brazenly stealing Ramrod's water and subsequently laying claim to it, had unwittingly provided them with a goat. What had Massey said last night? *When people start having trouble they start looking around for a goat.* They'd found their goat, but how far would they go?

Walt was not unacquainted with violence, for there was something basically violent in the way all cattlemen lived. They fought the elements, predators, conditions of grass and weather. Sometimes they fought among themselves over a variety of trivial things. But this was different, a smoldering kind of violence Walt had never known before.

He came into town, and headed at once toward the office of Sidney Bryce. It was located in a two-story building, the lower part of which housed the bank. You reached the office by an outside stairway.

Walt climbed the stairs, knowing he should have taken time to eat. A full stomach might have eased the run of his temper, but there seemed an urgency in him that could not be denied.

There was a landing at the top of the stairs and a door that was open this morning. He entered and went along a hall toward a sign that said: **Sidney Bryce—County Water Commissioner.** He passed the office of Peter Rider, an attorney, and Doc Curtis, who was the town's only doctor.

A hum of voices reached him from inside Bryce's office. He wondered briefly at it, then turned the knob and pushed open the door.

Bryce, a tall, middle-aged, bony man, sat at a cluttered

roll-top desk. His swivel chair was swung around, and he laid back in it chewing a pencil stub and staring at the crowd in the room. He turned his glance to Walt, but he didn't stir. His voice was deep and somehow harsh. "Come in, Walt. We were talking about you."

Walt pushed the door closed behind him and put his back to it. He glanced around at the men present. Some of them looked sheepish and embarrassed; some were brazen and defiant. But one attitude was common: they were all hostile. Walt felt that like a blow. He nodded at rodent-faced Hamp Richards and said: "You were a busy man last night, Hamp. You must've visited every place on Wild Horse Creek."

Hamp flushed, but he didn't speak. Walt saw Jess Armstrong's square, sullen face and he nodded to the man. "Hello, Jess."

He saw Wes Ordway, too, his head swathed with bandages. Wes had the irritability of pain stamped on his face.

Had Bryce's visitors been just these three, Walt would have thought nothing of it, assuming they were here to settle their disputed Rye Creek irrigation water. But there were others. There was Calvin Haley and Art Youra and Vic Lucero, Wild Horse Creek ranchers who had no interest in Rye Creek at all.

Walt said, more intemperately than he had intended: "Bryce, what the hell is the idea of giving Ramrod's water to Kenyon?"

Bryce's eyes grew hard at his tone. He countered: "Ramrod's water? It's Kenyon's water, Walt. You'll have to go to court to prove it's yours. And I doubt if you can do it."

For an instant an overpowering feeling of futility and defeat washed over Walt. The eyes of the men in the room looked at him coldly, holding an edge of satisfied gloating

70

as though it did their souls good to see the biggest rancher in the country humbled and defied.

Then anger replaced defeat in Walt. He could feel it rise through his body like a tide. He made a tight, small grin. He said rashly: "To hell with your god-damn' court, Bryce. That's Ramrod's water and Ramrod's going to have it. Today. With or without your approval."

Bryce actually seemed to smile, although it was a frosty mockery of a smile. He shrugged his bony shoulders, saying nothing. His eyes talked for him, saying: *Go ahead, Walt. Go ahead.*

Art Youra, his puffy face grim with indignation, turned his head toward the others. He spoke with a heavy, Slavic accent. "You hear? The courts of our country he curses." He looked at Hamp Richards. "You was right, Richards. Bigger than the law, they think they are. Bigger than the law, and full of greed. They must be stopped, if we our ranches wish to keep."

Youra turned and looked at Walt. His eyes were cold and surprisingly filled with hate.

Walt was, for the moment, appalled. He knew Art Youra. He'd eaten a number of times at Youra's house. He knew him as a jovial, good-hearted man who got along well with everybody.

Then courage took hold of Walt. He shouted, over the rising tide of indignant voices: "Wait a minute! Wait a minute! Hell, it isn't Ramrod that's stolen water! It's Kenyon!"

Youra faced him and asked coldly: "Is this not the thing for the court to say? Is it not Kenyon who now the water has?"

Walt nodded. "But. . . ."

Youra interrupted implacably. "Is it not Ramrod which

makes the threats to take it away from him? Is it not him, the water commissioner, who says this is not right?"

Walt looked at Youra helplessly. The room was now a babble of excited, angry voices. A low growl came from the throat of sullen, square-faced Jess Armstrong. The man stood hunched a little, as though only waiting a signal to attack. Walt thought unbelievingly: *This isn't possible! It can't be happening!*

But it was happening. These men, his friends and neighbors, had turned against him. In their faces he saw a number of things, none of which was pleasant. He saw hatred, dislike, suspicion, and distrust. And he saw something else, which disturbed him more than all the rest—a kind of eagerness. Suddenly he knew they wanted to destroy him. They wanted to destroy Ramrod.

It took a moment for his stunned mind to grasp the full meaning of what had happened, and they waited, like wolves ringing a bull in winter, to see what he would do.

Chapter Six

Walt's immediate inclination was to loose his fury upon them, to give voice to the full outrage of his indignation. He wanted to curse them, dare them to do their worst. Yet there was something that restrained him.

These were his friends and neighbors. He had quarreled with no single one of them in all his life. He had never done anything to hurt them, or to earn their hatred and hostility.

True, there had been a time when Ramrod, under Jake, was greedy and overbearing. Ramrod had squeezed several of the smaller ranches from their grass atop the plateau, and Bryce had been one of these. But, so far as Walt knew, none of the others facing him was among the ones Ramrod had squeezed.

He gazed hopelessly at the men in the room for a moment, knowing somehow that, if he provoked them now, this ugly thing that had begun in the valley would leap and grow beyond all bounds of reason. They wanted him to fight. They wanted an excuse to destroy him.

With his back to the door, and a trapped feeling in his mind, he said as calmly as he could: "This is crazy. Don't you realize how shaky Kenyon's claim to that water is? We gave him water, but never four and a half feet. He couldn't use that much on those postage stamp fields of his. And he's never done his share of the ditch work."

His words made no apparent impression on them. Youra nodded his head like a judge. He said with almost ludicrous solemnity: "Ya. Maybe Kenyon is too small to need water.

To decide it is for the court."

"But why are the rest of you mixing in? It's a dispute between Ramrod and Kenyon."

Armstrong said intemperately: "Yeah, an' when you're through with robbin' Kenyon, you'll turn to us. That's why we're mixin' in."

Walt said as patiently as he could: "We're not robbing Kenyon. He has robbed us. And how the hell could we start on you? Your water's adjudicated. Nobody can take it from you." He looked from one stony, implacable face to another. He tried not to see the hot eagerness in the eyes of Armstrong, Ordway, and Hamp Richards. Anger slipped into his voice as he said: "You know how long it takes a water case to get heard by a court. It'll take until spring. In the meantime, that water goes to waste, soaking up Kenyon's fields until they turn to swamps while Ramrod's hay crop burns out. Next winter we'll have to sell our herds. What good will the court's giving back the water do us then? We'll have lost even though we win."

He glanced at Bryce. Bryce looked as though he were trying hard not to smile. He said: "It's tough on you, Rand, but it's still a legal matter for a court to settle." There was an edge of triumph in his voice.

It grated on Walt, that triumph, more than anything that had gone before. For he knew that of all the men before him, only Bryce could be guilty of dishonesty. The others had nothing to gain and were driven, he was sure, by fear and helplessness in the face of heat and drought that threatened to rob them of everything they had.

Bryce was controlled by no such motivation. Bryce was using the authority of his office to incite the others and thus find satisfaction for his own hate. It was so obvious. It seemed suddenly of the greatest importance to Walt that the others also see what Bryce's motives were.

He crossed the room with two abrupt strides, brushing Youra and Armstrong aside. He seized Bryce by his shirt front and yanked him to his feet. His hand, striking Bryce's face, was like a series of closely spaced pistol shots.

He said between his teeth: "Talk, you son-of-a-bitch! Tell 'em the truth. Tell 'em why you're lying and why you're trying to wreck Ramrod!"

Bryce's face was white, red only where Walt's slaps had left their marks. He struggled silently, and suddenly the others surged upon Walt from behind. Armstrong's great fist struck him behind the ear. Hands clawed at him. They yanked him back, and his hands came away from Bryce with a tearing sound, clutching a piece of Bryce's shirt.

They all seemed to be hitting him at once in unplanned frenzy. He tried to whirl and face them, but one of his arms was held by Haley, the other by swarthy Vic Lucero. Armstrong kept beating at his face with both hands.

Walt bent convulsively and straightened like a whip. His head struck the wounded side of Ordway's head and the man went wild. Kicking, kneeing, he swarmed over Walt, his fists flying in a frenzied windmill fashion, some striking, some missing. In an instant blood was streaming from Walt's nose. His eyes felt puffy and numb. He brought a boot down on Ordway's instep and saw the man go to the floor. He kicked savagely, and left Ordway hugging his belly on the floor.

Hamp Richards, who had been hopping up and down with excitement, now gathered courage to step close and begin to kick at Walt. One of his boots caught Walt in the groin and pain spread agonizingly.

Bryce, who should have intervened, stood behind his desk, the faintest of smiles on his lined and weathered face. His eyes were cold as bits of stone.

They were all yelling, their shouts mingling, making an indecipherable bedlam from which occasionally an understandable cry would emerge. "Kill the son-of-a-bitch!" or "Beat the bastard so his wife won't know him!"

Furniture smashed under the impact of their bodies. The struggle roared from one end of the room to the other and back again. Walt fought as he'd never fought in his life, yanking and jerking at the restraining clutches on his arms, jackknifing his body convulsively when that failed.

Twice he tore lose and rolled to the floor, but each time they were on him again, smothering him, bearing him back to the floor with the weight of their numbers. Youra's frantic cry—"Wait! It is wrong, this!"—was lost in the racket and unheard by all but Walt.

The door splintered as they crashed against it, and they rolled out into the hall. Walt still fought like a demon, kicking, arching his body and butting them with his head. But he was growing weak. They were too many, and, although he inflicted hurts upon each of them, the hurts they inflicted upon him were greater.

Armstrong held him now, kneeing him in the small of the back. Ordway's hands were around his throat, choking off his breath. Hamp Richards began to pummel his unprotected face, grunting with each blow, sweating profusely and wild of eye.

Down the hall they surged, banging against first one wall and then the other. Rider, the attorney, looked out, then slammed and locked his door. Doc Curtis didn't even open his. He knew they'd come in for him when the fight was done.

The screen door leading to the landing gave before them. They rolled onto the landing and the rail cracked and sagged. Frightened, they all pulled back, dragging Walt with them.

Hamp Richards began to yell: "Throw 'im down the stairs! That'll cool 'im off." He was breathing as though he had run a mile.

Youra stood there, and Walt caught a fleeting glimpse of excited indignation. "It is wrong, this! Law-abiding men we are. Stop it! Stop, I say!"

It was as though he had not spoken. Walt heard him, but he doubted if the others did. The blows didn't hurt so much now. His head reeled and felt very light. His body was almost numb.

They dragged him toward the door again, intending, no doubt, to follow Hamp's advice.

Youra stood there, and Walt caught a fleeting glimpse of him before he was whirled around. Youra held a double-barreled shotgun in his hands. Where he'd got it, Walt didn't know. Probably in Bryce's office.

There was steel in Youra's voice as he yelled again: "Stop it! Stop, or I shoot!"

They paid no heed. The blast of the shotgun was like a rush of hot air against them. The charge passed over their heads and tore into the ceiling. Plaster rained on the struggling men. Acrid, black powder smoke filled the corridor.

They froze, their struggles at an end. Still holding Walt, they looked toward the doorway onto the landing.

Youra had lowered the muzzle of the gun. "One barrel left I have," he said. "Let him go or I shoot."

They released Walt, and he sagged against the wall. It took all the will he had to remain upright. Youra said, moving out of the door but keeping the unwavering muzzle of the gun on them: "Now go! To your homes go. It is ashamed you should be."

Walt had never seen Youra this way. Youra had always seemed a harmless, ineffectual man, good at growing things and not much else. The steel in Youra surprised him now, as it no doubt surprised the others. They grumbled, but they filed past Youra one by one and clumped down the stairs to the street.

Youra broke the shotgun and stood it in the corner by the door. He looked at Walt coldly, no trace of sympathy in his face. He said: "You I do not like. You are a thief. But in the law I believe. Go now to the doctor. He will patch you up." He turned and followed the others down the stairs.

Walt had the oddest, most overpowering inclination to laugh. Instead, he felt his eyes fill with tears. He shook his head angrily.

Piled atop the hurts of last night, the hurts of today became almost unbearable. There was not a square inch of his body that didn't ache. Blood still welled from his nose and from an inch-long gash on his cheek bone. It matted his beard stubble and spotted the front of his shirt. His shirt was torn and he was covered with the dirt from the oiled wooden floor. He debated refusing Doc Curtis's attentions, then changed his mind. He staggered along the hall toward Doc's door.

He went in without knocking. Doc Curtis was a squat, swarthy man, one of the most incredibly ugly men Walt had ever known. His manner was brusque but his eyes were not. He said: "Collapse on that couch, Walt. Christ, they kicked hell out of you, didn't they? What was it all about?"

Walt didn't answer. He laid back on the couch and let Doc go to work on his face. Alcohol was a biting smell in his nostrils and a sharp, burning pain in the cuts on his face that made him wince. When his face was clean, Doc took a couple of expert, quick stitches in the largest of the cuts, that on his cheek bone.

Then he unbuttoned Walt's shirt and examined his bruises. Unexpectedly he got a bottle of liniment and began to rub Walt's muscles. His hands were big and stubby and strong and, although they didn't hurt, they brought a glowing warmth to Walt's body that made the pain seem less. When he was finished, he rolled Walt over and did his back.

Walt kept turning Doc's question over in his mind. What *had* it been about? Certainly not water. It was an amazing, incomprehensible, frightening thing. Those men had made Walt a symbol, just as the Salem witch burners had made their innocent victims symbols of evil. And yet, exactly what had they made Walt a symbol of?

He shook his head wearily. It was beyond understanding and there was no use trying to understand it. Probably the men themselves could not understand it, much less explain it.

Doc finished, and Walt stood up. He groaned. He made it to his feet, waited until the dizziness passed, then buttoned his shirt wherever the buttons had not been torn off. Doc said seriously: "Don't let them get you again, boy. Next time they'll kill you."

Walt shook his head numbly. There was growing in him an altogether new kind of anger that was cold and steady and dangerous. It was not the irritable anger of yesterday, not the burning rage he'd felt toward Kenyon during their fight. It was something altogether different.

He said: "They'll not get me again, Doc."

Doc Curtis stared at him for a moment and turned away.

Walt went out into the hall. His hat was lying just inside the broken door to Bryce's office. Walt went over and picked it up. When he straightened, he looked at Bryce, who was helplessly surveying the damage to his office. Half the furniture was smashed, and papers were strewn from one end of it to the other.

Walt said quietly: "Back away, Bryce. Back away from this thing or I'm going to kill you."

He stared at Bryce a moment more, then turned and limped down the hallway toward the landing.

Chapter Seven

He paused on the landing as the sun glare struck and dazzled him. He blinked a couple of times, then reached up and pulled his hat forward to shade his eyes. He held firmly to the rail as he went down, dizzy and sick. At the bottom he paused again, looking up and down the street.

He saw none of the men who had attacked him. A woman was just coming out of Massey's store, leading a boy by the hand. Walt went that way, and passed her on the walk. She was Lew Purdy's wife, and she looked at him in the gentle, shocked, reproving way she had for anyone bearing the marks of violence.

John Massey was behind the counter. Walt said: "I want five sticks of dynamite, half a dozen caps, and six or eight feet of fuse."

Massey hesitated.

Walt said: "John, don't interfere. I know what I'm doing."

Massey looked at Walt in exactly the same way Doc Curtis had looked at him before he had turned away. He went to the back of the store. Walt followed. Massey went out the door and across the yard, with Walt a few feet behind. He unlocked the door to a small shed and got the dynamite from a box with its top pried off. He slipped it into a paper sack, found caps, and handed them to Walt. "Put those in your shirt pocket. Don't ever keep 'em with the powder." He unrolled a length of fuse and cut it off.

Walt said: "How much?"

"Fifty cents."

Walt paid him. He took the dynamite and the fuse and, without returning to the store, walked up the alley until he came to the street. He could feel John Massey's eyes on him all the way and sensed Massey's disapproval.

He cut over to Main again, and entered Sally Croft's restaurant. The place was empty, so he took a stool at the counter. Sally called—"Just a minute!"—from the kitchen, and appeared a moment later brushing a damp wisp of hair from her forehead.

She was younger than he but had been in the same grade at school. There was always considerable good-natured kidding between them, but this morning her eyes were grave. "Walt, what's the matter? What's happening to this town?"

He managed a grin and looked up into her plain, flushed face. There was a slight beading of sweat on her upper lip. He said: "I don't know one damned thing more about it than you do, Sally. I just happened to be the one that caught all the hell. Rustle me up some ham and eggs, will you? And about a gallon of coffee to start off with."

"Sure, Walt." She turned and went to the kitchen, returning a moment later with a thick mug of coffee. He sipped it black, and it was like fire on his bruised mouth. He got up and wandered behind the counter, where he got a fresh sack of tobacco and a packet of papers. He rolled a cigarette carefully, stuck it in his mouth, and lighted it. He remembered the dynamite caps and buttoned his pocket over them. He tried not to think of Kenyon, Armstrong, Ordway, and Hamp, because thinking of them did something unpleasant to his stomach.

He could hear Sally moving about in the kitchen. He heard the eggs sizzle as she dropped them into the pan. Heat rolled out of the kitchen, and Walt could feel sweat rolling across his chest and gathering on his forehead. Although it made him sweat worse, he finished the coffee.

Sally brought him his ham and eggs, and Walt forced himself to eat. Food nauseated him, but he successfully got it all down in spite of both the nausea and his bruised and swelling mouth. One of his eyes was swelling, too, and he supposed it would close before it stopped.

She stood watching him all the time, her eyes holding a mixture of emotions it was hard for him to understand. He supposed Sally knew everything that had happened just as everyone in town undoubtedly did. News traveled fast in a small community.

Sally asked as he finished: "What will you do now, Walt?"

He looked up and grinned crookedly. "What does any man do when something has been stolen from him? He tries to get it back. That's what I'm going to do."

He paid for his meal and the tobacco. He picked up his paper sack, tipped his hat down over his eyes, and stepped out the door into the sunlight. In spite of the heat inside the restaurant, stepping outside was like stepping into an oven and it was not yet noon.

The street was almost ankle-deep with powdery dust, but no wind stirred it up. A heat haze lay in the valley north of town, and rising layers of heat made the plateau shimmer oddly as though viewed through a cheap pane of glass. The sky was cloudless and the color of brass.

A lone man was cutting diagonally across the street in front of the Stockmen's Bank, but he was not one of those who had attacked Walt. Otherwise, the street was deserted save for two panting dogs sniffing warily at each other.

Walt walked toward the rail in front of the bank, where his horse waited dejectedly. The animal's head was down, his only movement that of his tail, switching at flies.

There was a certain defiance in Walt and no fear as he stood at his horse's head and surveyed the street of the town. Although he was no better equipped to fight them now, he would have welcomed their return. A strange, light feeling in his head and that steady, implacable anger in his heart made striking back a virtual necessity for him.

But no one appeared, so at last he mounted and reined around. He glanced up at Bryce's office window and saw the man withdraw his face from it hastily. The curtain dropped back into place.

Walt headed for the valley road. He had almost reached it when he heard galloping hoofs in the dusty street behind him. He turned his head and saw Irish McKeogh hurrying to overtake him on his blocky dappled gray. Walt reined in.

Irish was scowling. In his eyes, besides anger, Walt thought he saw what almost amounted to desperation. Irish asked the same question Sally had asked: "What are you going to do?"

Walt looked at him for a moment. He had always liked Irish and considered him a father-in-law, although his real relationship was that of uncle-in-law. Yet now Walt felt truculence rising in him. He said: "What I should have done yesterday when I came off the mountain. I'm going to get our water back."

Irish stared at him. "For your own damned good I ought to throw you in jail. You won't live three days the way you're going."

Walt grinned and winced because it hurt. He said: "Don't try it, Irish."

Wrath flared in Irish McKeogh's eyes. "And don't you tell me my business." He quieted his temper with a visible effort. He said: "I mean it, Walt. Keep going and some-body's going to kill you."

"They're not going to find me so easy next time." He glared at Irish. "Tell me, Irish, isn't it the sheriff's job to enforce the law and keep the peace? Where were you when that bunch was working me over?"

Irish flushed angrily. "I can't be everywhere at once. You know that. Besides, you weren't in the right. You attacked Bryce."

Walt said: "You're hiding behind half-truths and you know it. Let's not talk about right and wrong if you can't be more honest than that."

Irish had been flushed before. Now he turned almost purple.

Walt said—"Think on it."—gave his back to Irish and touched his horse's sides with the spurred heels. The horse broke into a jogging trot. Walt wanted to look around at Irish, but he kept his eyes straight ahead.

He couldn't help feeling sympathy for the sheriff. Irish had never come up against anything quite like this before. He was as appalled as Walt by it, and he was too smart a man to sit back and try to delude himself into believing it would blow over. It wouldn't. Instead, it would grow until half the men in the valley had themselves believing it would be a public service to eliminate Walt and destroy Ramrod.

A spot on Walt's back suddenly became inordinately sensitive, as though he expected a bullet to strike him. He fought down an impulse to glance around.

He scoffed at himself, but he knew that many a man had been dry-gulched over less than the trouble brewing here in Wild Horse Valley. In an arid country, water was life. Without it, ranches failed and men went broke. Walt guessed there had been more violence generated by water disputes than by any other single cause.

This had grown into more than a water dispute. It had somehow grown into something personal, a struggle between those who had nothing and Ramrod, which, to their way of thinking, had everything. All the smoldering jealousies and resentments for a score of years were involved.

There were some who would accuse Ramrod of stealing from Kenyon that which was rightfully his. Still others would say that Ramrod had stolen directly from them over the past thirty years by giving water to Kenyon which should, rightfully, have been returned to the creek for use by others farther down its course, and so they would involve themselves in the dispute.

Jake's conduct, more than fifteen years ago, would come under their scrutiny, and upon Walt would fall the blame for Jake's seizure of range even though he'd been only a boy at the time.

Walt passed the Guilfoile place and saw Tommy down in the yard a hundred yards from the road working on a dump rake. Tommy glanced up. He half raised a hand to wave, then glanced quickly at the house. He yanked his hand down and bent over his work. He did not look up again.

Walt had raised his own hand and waved to Tommy. He dropped it with a vague feeling of embarrassment.

Up to now, he had felt only anger and outrage at the things that happened. Now he knew a feeling of hurt. Tommy had not failed to recognize him, nor had he failed to see Walt's wave. Walt thought bitterly: *They can't even keep the kids out of it.*

He had a trapped and almost frantic feeling as he continued on to Ramrod. It was as though he were a leper, stoned and driven away by those who had been his friends, and he had done nothing at all to deserve it.

He tied his horse to the same verandah post he had used yesterday, a little startled to realize that everything that had happened had occurred in less than twenty-four hours.

He laid the sack of dynamite on the porch, then went across toward the door. He hated to face Jake in his present mood and found little pleasure even in thinking of Rose. But he couldn't go, unarmed, to Kenyon's place for the job he had to do.

The door opened, even as he reached for the knob. Rose stood in it, staring at him in dismay. "Walt! What's happening now? What's happening to you?"

He was instantly defensive. "Happening to me? Nothing, except that I'm getting god-damned mad." He yanked upon the screen door and stepped inside.

His left eye was almost closed now. His right was bruised and turning black, but the swelling was not severe.

He glared at his wife, feeling more alone than ever before in his life. He wanted her approval, yet somehow thought she should give it instinctively. He shouldn't have to beg for it.

He stepped over to the coat closet and reached inside. A little defiant because of embarrassment, he withdrew the cartridge belt and holstered .45, dusted them with a bandanna. Then he hung the belt around his waist and buckled it.

He avoided Rose's eyes. He'd worn this thing pretty proudly when he was eighteen. He'd taken it off at twenty and hadn't worn it since. He felt self-conscious wearing it, juvenile and foolish.

Her voice was suddenly calm, and filled with concern. "Wait, sit down. You and I have to talk. I don't know what's happening and I've got to know. I'm frightened."

He looked at her. She *was* frightened. Her face was white and scared. He felt a surge of protectiveness and love.

He sat down abruptly, feeling the weakness of the battering he had received. He said: "I went to town to see Bryce. You knew I was going to do that. I went to his office and there were six or seven of the small ranchers there . . . Haley, Youra, Lucero, Armstrong, Ordway, and Hamp Richards."

"And they did this to you? Why?"

He looked at her. "I don't know why. They've picked up this squabble between Kenyon and us and made it their own fight. By God, Rose, they act as if it was some kind of crusade."

"Walt, I don't understand."

He frowned. "How could you? I don't understand it myself. Maybe it's the heat, or the drought, or both of them. Maybe they're scared. Maybe it's as John Massey said, that, when people get scared, they start looking around for a goat. But I've been their goat long enough. They can start looking around for another one."

"What's the gun for?" She whispered the words and waited breathlessly for his answer.

He opened his mouth to speak, but was interrupted by Jake's mocking cackle from across the room. How long Jake had been there he had no way of knowing. There was a rug runner in the hall and Jake could have approached silently in spite of the metal wheels of his wheelchair.

Jake said: "The gun, Rose, is to kill that thievin' sweetie of yours, Kenyon."

Rose whirled around, her face flaming.

Jake laughed again. "That is, if he's got the guts to use it, which I doubt."

Wild fury flared like a grass fire in Walt. He clenched his fists tightly between his knees. For an instant he trembled with the effort he made to control himself. Then he spoke between his teeth: "Rose, go pack yourself a bag. You're going down and stay with Irish for a while. I've had enough of this."

Without looking either at Rose or Jake, he got up and banged out the door. He untied his horse, snatched up his paper sack, and flung himself into his saddle. He heard Rose crying on the porch behind him, but he didn't stop.

Chapter Eight

Riding up the lane toward the road, Walt stared upward at the lofty, precipitous rim that guarded the plateau. In some places it was a full five hundred feet high, but in others narrowed down to forty or fifty feet. The trail where Walt had come off yesterday ascended through one such narrow spot and was plainly visible from here, a zigzag thread like a spider web trailing from the dark fringe of spruce above the rim.

His glance swung upcountry toward the headwaters of Wild Horse Creek. There, where rims petered out altogether and the country gradually flattened as the valley rose to join the plateau, clouds hung, puffy and white, idle and without threat of rain. Farther west, shrouded by the mists of distance, he could vaguely see the country that fed Rye Creek, and over this vast area clouds also hung. He thought once more: *Why the hell doesn't it rain?*

Perhaps a rain wouldn't solve Ramrod's problems. Perhaps it wouldn't settle the quarrel Ramrod had with Kenyon, or the never-ending quarrel Walt seemed to have with his father. But it would ease problems for all the others who lived under the shadow of the great plateau. It would fill their streams with a muddy torrent that they could divert into their ditches and onto their burning fields. It would take them out of Walt's quarrel with Kenyon. Without interference, he could settle that himself.

He opened the gate without dismounting, rode through, and closed it behind him. He put his horse into a steady trot and headed north. Looking back, he could see Rose standing on the verandah, shading her eyes with an upraised hand as she stared worriedly after him.

He began to sweat profusely. Sun heat rose from the hard-packed road in shimmering waves that created mirages ahead, mirages that looked like pools of cool water lying in each low place in the road. And he began to wonder about Rose. Was she happy? Was she satisfied with her life at Ramrod as Walt Rand's wife? He frowned. Or had she, indeed, accepted him as a kind of consolation prize after Claude's untimely death? Could it be that she wanted Kenyon?

A tiny gray lizard streaked across the road and paused at its edge to watch Walt with beady, unblinking eyes. High up in the sky a hawk wheeled and soared. Walt's thoughts and doubts went on.

He swung his gaze from Rose to Kenyon's house, nestling almost hidden in a grove of cottonwoods. He wasn't afraid of Kenyon, but he knew the temper of the man. He knew that jealousy was galling Kenyon and that, furthermore, Kenyon would be smarting over the beating Walt had given him the night before. Kenyon, today, would be capable of using a rifle to keep Walt away from the head gate in the ditch.

He fingered the sack containing the dynamite and fuse. It rattled dryly. He unbuttoned his shirt pocket and peered down at the dynamite caps. They were small cylinders of brass, less than the diameter of a pencil and about an inch and a half long. Although they looked harmless, Walt knew that six of them, if detonated all at once, had the power to blow half his chest away.

He turned in at Kenyon's gate, just outside comfortable rifle range, but feeling jittery just the same. Chances were, a first shot from the house would miss, for the range was over three hundred yards. But Kenyon could be lucky.

Caution made Walt eye the wide-swinging route toward the head gate, but perverse stubbornness made him take the shorter, more direct route that came within a hundred yards of the house. Sweat stung the cuts on his face. An ache began in the middle of his chest and spread until it seemed to encompass his entire body.

His decision was made, yet doubt still rode him. Irish had warned him not to take his water back by force. Bryce had warned him similarly. The six in Bryce's office had warned him with their blows if not with their words. Anger stirred as he thought of that. There was one way and only one that a man could answer such brutal intimidation. This was Walt's way, the only one that he could see.

Walt's horse sank fetlock deep in the soil of Kenyon's fields. He could hear the gurgle of water running. Down at the lower end, where the field was flat, he could see a lake already beginning to form, water wasted, that would lie and grow stagnant, breeding mosquitoes and polliwogs until the dry air sucked it up and left nothing behind but the cracked earth to show for its presence.

The heat, increased here by humid air, seemed to beat against Walt with a menacing strength. Out of the corner of his eye he glanced at Kenyon's house, now scarcely more than a hundred yards away. He looked ahead at the point where he would be closest to the house, and then onward to the point of willows behind where safety lay.

His eye caught the glint of sun on steel at Kenyon's open window, and his muscles bunched beneath him. His horse perhaps felt this for he increased his pace. Walt deliberately reined him in.

Stopped, he turned to stare at the house, saying plainly

by his stance: *You'll never get a better chance, Kenyon. If you're going to shoot, shoot now.*

But no shot came. Seconds ran on and became minutes, and at last Walt touched heels to his horse's sides and sighed out with vast relief.

He did not delude himself that the danger was past. It wasn't. Kenyon had simply refused to shoot him without provocation. When the head gate blew. . . .

At the head gate, Walt dismounted and dropped his horse's reins. He looked up again toward the house. It was visible through a break in the willows and about two hundred and fifty yards away.

Walt leaped across the ditch, which was nearly five feet wide. On the other side he knelt and removed the dynamite from the sack. Laying it carefully on the ground, he returned to his horse and with his pocket knife cut one of the saddle thongs. He divided it and cut it in two, then leaped the ditch again.

He tied the dynamite with the two pieces of thong into two bundles, one of three sticks, one of two. Then he cut the fuse in half.

He crimped a cap onto the end of each length of fuse with his teeth. Then, tearing a bit of the paper from around a stick in each bundle of dynamite, he inserted the caps, burying them in the yielding, clay-like substance of the explosive.

Occasionally he glanced up at the house. When he was finished, he lowered one bundle of dynamite into the water ahead of the head gate. If the underwater charge blew, it would destroy the bundle left above water. If it didn't, he'd light the second one and destroy the head gate from above water.

With a final glance at the house, he thumbed a match

alight and touched it to the fuse of the underwater charge. It did not catch immediately, and he realized he should have cut the end cleanly, then frayed it with a thumbnail. He fumbled for his knife that he had returned to his pocket. He glanced at Kenyon's house.

He saw the mushrooming muzzle smoke of Kenyon's rifle before he heard either bullet or report. He tried to fling himself sideways knowing even as he did that it was too late.

The bullet struck the water behind him in the ditch with a sound like that of a flat board striking a horse's rump and raised a spray that fanned out over the ditch like a fountain. Then Walt was flat on his belly, his head against the earth. The report reached him, flat and wicked and deadly, while the spray raised by the bullet was still settling down.

A chill began in Walt's spine as he realized what path that bullet must have taken to strike the water in the ditch behind him. It had to have been aimed directly at his chest, and it could not have missed by more than a few inches or it would not have struck inside the ditch.

Cautiously he raised his head. His face was still and without expression. His eyes, although holding a kind of incredulous shock, were cold. Kenyon had not tried to discourage him, or tried to drive him away. Kenyon had deliberately and cold-bloodedly tried to kill him.

Here he lay, exposed to the house if he so much as raised his head. He glanced around. His horse had spooked away from the sound of the bullet striking and now stood with his ears laid back a dozen yards away. Between Walt and the horse was almost thirty feet of open ground, where he would be fully exposed.

He did not delude himself that Kenyon would let him reach his horse. Kenyon, by that deliberately aimed shot, had committed himself irrevocably to killing Walt, and, now that he was committed in his own mind, Kenyon would not give up.

Walt reached back and felt the smooth grips of his revolver. Bitterness touched him. At this range, the revolver was about as effective as a slingshot. Walt doubted if it would even reach close enough to Kenyon to make the man duck his head.

The rifle roared again, and this time the bullet tore away a chunk of the head gate not six inches from the tied bundle of dynamite.

Every nerve in his body screamed for him to retreat. By wriggling back, he could stay partially covered by the ditch bank until he reached the willows. Then he could make his way back to Ramrod afoot.

This would have been the easy way, yet Walt knew, if he took it, he was done. Kenyon would have him on the run and would forever keep him running. Nor was it this realization alone that made him stay. There was anger, cold and implacable but steady as a bed of glowing coals. There was a consciousness of being in the right. There was stubbornness. This was Ramrod's water and he meant to have it. He raised his head and saw the muzzle bloom again in the window of the house. He resisted the impulse to duck, but he heard the buzzing whine of the bullet's passing overhead.

Immediately, then, he lunged up the bank. He cut the fuse end and frayed it with his thumbnail. Then he flung backward, rolling.

Kenyon's bullet again tore a chunk from the head gate, although this one was almost a foot from the exposed charge.

Walt raised up to draw another shot, dropping almost immediately. He heard the report as he thumbed his match alight. He clawed forward and laid the flaring match against the fraying end of the fuse.

The rifle roared and Walt flinched as the bullet struck the ditch bank and flung up a blinding shower of dust and dirt. His legs straightened convulsively under him and he fell backward, rolling. Glancing back, he saw a thin plume of smoke curling up from the end of the fuse. The powder inside the fuse hadn't caught yet, but the tarry, frayed end had. Perhaps it would spread and catch the fuse itself.

It did, as he watched. A thin jet of fire sprayed from the end of the fuse. Now, it was cover he needed, and distance from the blast.

He lunged to his feet, running. His boots dug into the dry soil, flinging back little spurts of dust. He ran, half bent over, off balance and falling. The rifle roared spitefully, but the bullet *buzzed* harmlessly overhead.

Then Walt fell. He lay still, his arms hugging his head and covering his ears against the concussion of the blast. He hoped there was enough distance between himself and the ditch, and that the first blast wouldn't fling the second charge his way.

The waiting seemed hours instead of a few short minutes. The rifle kept barking, and the bullets kept striking near, each time flinging up a shower of dirt and each time whining off into the distance upcountry.

Walt's first consciousness of the blast itself was communicated to his body by the ground upon which he lay. It trembled briefly, as though the earth under him were stirring and about to erupt. Then the air was filled with sound, a deep, terrifying rumble of sound that beat upon his eardrums, whipped his clothing, and made his breathing stop.

The sound of the actual blast lasted but a moment, although the moment seemed to stretch into hours. Following it was a rushing sound of planks and water and mud flying in all directions, and then the rain began. Water and mud rained down on Walt and drenched him instantly. A bit of plank landed on his back and made him grunt. He swung his head to look and a gob of mud struck him in the face.

Then there was silence, a silence so vast it was as terrifying in its way as the blast had been. Even the rifle up at the house was still.

Walt's horse, as the blast went off, stood still for the briefest instant. Then he began to buck. He started to run toward the road, away from the ditch, but a bit of flying plank struck him on the nose and turned him back, so that now, looking toward him, Walt saw that he was almost to the ditch, running as though he was out of his mind with fear.

Walt came to his hands and knees, thinking he would seize the horse's dangling reins as the animal leaped the ditch and went on past. The rifle barked spitefully. The bullet struck the cinch flinch. It was not at Walt that the rifle had been aimed.

The horse's head went down as though he had been pole-axed. He seemed to stumble, and then was rolling end over end, a flying welter of head and tail and hoofs. He rolled into the ditch with a gigantic splash, spraying Walt with water and further drenching him, and came to rest as though lying down against the near bank of the ditch. His head, held up for an instant, fell back against the ditch bank. Awareness faded from the horse's eyes and they became glassy and blank.

The rifle barked again and Walt felt it tug at the crown of his hat, which miraculously had stayed on his head. There was nowhere he could go except into the ditch, and he went in without hesitation.

The head gate was gone altogether. Water flowed past the place it had been, heading toward Ramrod again. The level of water had dropped in the ditch so that now water was running back toward the head gate out of Kenyon's ditch.

Walt reached under the horse and cut the cinch, losing his knife in the process. He stripped his bridle from the horse's head, then heaved both saddle and bridle out of the ditch. He followed them, rolling, drenched to the skin and wondering why it seemed so important to him to recover his saddle and bridle.

The rifle barked spitefully. The bullet struck the cinch ring with a sharp, *clanging* sound, then ricocheted away with a high, diminishing whine.

Before Kenyon could shoot again, Walt was up, hampered by the saddle he was lugging but as stubborn about that now as he had been a few moments before about the head gate. It seemed inordinately important to him that Kenyon should take nothing from him in retaliation for the destruction of the head gate.

A bullet tore through his saddle, which Walt held between himself and the house, tearing a hole Walt could have put his fist through. Splinters from the saddletree penetrated his leg over a spot as big as the palm of his hand. For a moment he thought he had been struck by the bullet, but his legs continued to pump frantically and he realized at last, with relief, that they would have been unable to do so had the bullet struck one of them.

Then he was behind the cover of willows, and he dropped both saddle and bridle and fell to the ground, gasping for breath. For a few moments he lay still, dragging air into his lungs in great, sighing gasps. His leg stung savagely where the splinters had torn into it. He knew he'd spend a good half hour with the tweezers before he got them out. But it was a small price to pay for the result he had accomplished.

He grinned and stood up, careful to keep the willows between himself and the house. He looked toward the ditch, toward the place where the head gate had been.

Water ran again in Ramrod's ditches. It would be days before Kenyon could replace the head gate, even with a dam, and he'd never be able to replace it unless Ramrod wanted him to. A single man could sit over there on the cedar-covered hills with a rifle and keep Kenyon from working. Walt edged around through the willows and peered at the house. He was in time to see Kenyon leave, heading down into the creek bottom, the rifle in his hand.

So it wasn't over yet. Kenyon was between Walt and the house at Ramrod, and Kenyon had a rifle while Walt had only his revolver.

He dragged it from the holster and looked at it. No use replacing the cartridges. The ones in his belt were just as wet. Checking it, he fired it once into the air. Then, satisfied, he picked up the saddle and bridle and headed down the dry bed of the creek.

Chapter Nine

As Walt traveled, he became increasingly aware that his stubbornness in regard to the saddle, if continued, could well cost him his life. Stealth, in traveling through the willows and thorny locusts that lined the creek, would be well nigh impossible with the saddle across his shoulder. It was ruined anyway. Kenyon's bullet, a soft-nosed hunting bullet, had damaged it beyond repair.

Accordingly Walt reluctantly cached the saddle and bridle in the crotch of a tree, and went on without it, immeasurably relieved. His revolver was in his hand, reloaded and with the hammer cocked. He supposed Kenyon had concealed himself at some spot that would overlook the creek bottom. Chances were that the first indication Walt would have of his location would come through a smashing slug from his rifle.

One of those hunting bullets could tear hell out of a man. They spread on contact, mushrooming as they traveled. Often they shattered upon contact with a bone, so that even a normally non-fatal wound became fatal. Walt had seen too often what a soft-nosed slug would do to a deer not to have a chill of dread run down his spine at the thought of what one slug might do to him. Still, he was damned if he'd give Kenyon the satisfaction of seeing him run upcountry.

The very thought of running upcountry gave Walt an idea. He began to grin coldly. Thereafter, he searched around with his eyes until he found a spot that, like Kenyon's, commanded a good view of the creek bottom. He went to it and sat down comfortably to wait.

As he waited, he considered with shocked puzzlement all that had happened in the past twenty-four hours. It appalled him to realize that Kenyon hated him enough deliberately to plan his death. Yet that was the only reasonable explanation for Kenyon's theft of water that he could have had practically for the asking. Kenyon's hatred must have grown out of jealousy. But why had it grown with such apparent suddenness?

Walt considered that, and decided Kenyon's hatred could not possibly have grown this suddenly. Yet, if it hadn't, the man was certainly a master at concealing his feelings. There wasn't a week went past when Walt didn't see Kenyon at least once, to lend him machinery, to give him water, to help him hay, or for any one of a hundred other small reasons. Kenyon had always been sullen, but Walt had supposed that was the man's actual way. Now he guessed there had been more to it than sullenness all along.

Walt considered the possibility that Jake had been responsible, either directly or indirectly, for Olaf Kenyon's death. Jake had exhibited more agitation over Walt's questioning him about Olaf Kenyon than he ever had over anything else. Perhaps they had fought. Perhaps, even, Jake had killed Olaf. If he had, Olaf's son Nick could scarcely be blamed for his hating Jake, and Ramrod, and even Jake's son. But it seemed odd that Kenyon's hatred had not become apparent before now. Walt scowled. Obviously Kenyon wanted Rose. But good Lord, was the man willing to kill for her?

A branch cracked a hundred feet downstream from where Walt sat. He froze, his head turned toward the sound. He came face to face with a question that needed answering in his own mind. Was he prepared to kill Kenyon, even in self-defense? He realized he was not—if killing could be avoided.

Another branch cracked, closer this time. Walt strained his eyes, looking toward the sound, but he saw nothing.

Instinctively he crouched closer to the ground, concealing himself behind the screening underbrush. The sun beat against his back like the glare from a furnace and in the still air close to the ground sweat poured from his body in spite of the cooling action of his damp clothes. His gun was thrust out before him and his eyes were narrowed against the glare. His beard itched and he scratched it idly with his free hand.

An interminable time passed and uneasiness ran through Walt. Had Kenyon seen him? Was he even now circling, coming upon Walt from the rear so he'd have a clear and unobstructed shot?

Walt swung his head and peered behind him. Irritability and anger began to grow in him again. What the hell was he doing here, crouched in the brush while another man hunted him like an animal? What had he done that this should happen to him?

He stirred uncomfortably. There was a strange compulsion in him to stand and show himself, to call out and have this done once and for all.

He thought of Bryce and of Irish McKeogh. If Walt killed Kenyon, Bryce would have a warrant out for him as soon as the news hit town. Irish would have to serve it. Walt shook his head almost imperceptibly.

He waited almost half an hour more, but heard no further sounds. Judging that Kenyon was now out of sight upstream, Walt rose stiffly to his feet.

A hundred yards upstream a rifle cracked. The bullet shattered a locust branch beside Walt's head and a thorn raked his face as the branch fell.

He started violently as the rifle crashed. Then he whirled

and triggered an undirected shot in the general direction of the rifle shot. The rifle roared again. Apparently Kenyon could not see Walt clearly or he'd have hit him before now.

Walt didn't wait until Kenyon could see him. Even a hundred yards was too long a range for a short-barreled revolver. Walt plunged away, his legs driving like locomotive pistons.

He crashed through the thorny locusts. His foot caught on a root and he sprawled headlong. Rising immediately, he went on. He reached a clearing and sprinted across it.

He hurt from the fall. His bruised body was wrenched and strained. The thorny locusts raked his face and hands as he plunged through them. He paused for breath and turned to face the direction of this man who was hunting him like a predator through the brush.

His eyes were angry slits of red. His words were the merest, breathless whisper. "Don't push it too far, Kenyon."

The fight he fought now was within himself. It galled him to run like a bullet-burned coyote, his tail between his legs. Anger at his position was a thrusting, driving force in his mind. He thought: *I'll run today, Kenyon. But don't cross the line onto Ramrod. If you do, you're a dead man.*

Traveling through the brush-choked creek bottom, he reached the house at Ramrod in late afternoon without further incident. He stopped at the watering trough and sloshed water over his face and head. On the back porch he grabbed a towel hanging over the washstand there and dried his face and hands. He stepped inside the kitchen door.

The kitchen was very hot, for there was a fire going in the stove. The air was strong with the aroma of spice cookies. Rose, in the middle of lifting a pan of them from the oven, straightened as he came in. The face she turned toward him was flushed and damp from the heat of the stove. It was her eyes that caught and held his glance. In them was the expression a thousand generations of women have shown their returning men—relief so intense it was almost an agony.

Tears sprang into them at once. She set the pan of cookies down on the tabletop. He stepped toward her, but something in her face warned him away.

She said: "I heard the dynamite. Then I heard the rifle shots. I heard you fire twice."

He waited.

After a moment she asked: "Can you understand what a woman goes through when she thinks her man is dead?" He opened his mouth to speak, but she cut him short: "Have you got your precious water back?"

He nodded.

She asked: "Is a stream of water worth dying for?"

She was hurt and scared and right now needed nothing so much as the strength of his arms around her. He knew that and so did she, but both knew as well that it was not the time.

He picked up a cookie, and took a bite. "These are good." He finished the cookie with her looking at him oddly, and at last met her glance. "There's a hell of a lot more to it than a stream of water, Rose. The water is only an excuse. Kenyon wants to kill me."

"I don't believe that, Walt. Why should he suddenly want to kill you? You've been neighbors with him for years. Why should he decide this week that he wants to kill you?"

The coolness that had developed between them this morning was present again. Walt looked at her coldly and she returned his glance with equal coldness.

Walt said: "You want to believe that Kenyon's right.

You want to believe that I'm wrong. Why?"

Her eyes were, for a moment, almost desperate, but her voice was steady. "You're saying something with your mind, Walt, that you're not quite putting into words."

He had the feeling, the illusion perhaps, that she was moving further and further away from him as the moments passed. Suddenly his arms went out. His big hands caught her shoulders and pulled her against him. He looked down at the top of her shining head. He said frantically: "Rose, they're trying to wreck me. But I can't lose you. I can't! I'll give them Ramrod before I'll let you slip away."

She looked up, her eyes big. "Would you, Walt?"

"I said it, didn't I?"

Damn, he thought, *what's the matter with us?* It was as though a wall stood between them that both wanted to scale, but that neither could. They were touchy with heat and trouble and fear.

He heard the tires of Jake's wheelchair approaching. He released Rose and looked toward the door with open hostility. That was part of the trouble, damn it. If Rose and he could ever finish a discussion, maybe they'd get it settled between them. The way it was, Jake always butted in before they could.

Jake rolled in, saying as he came through the door: "I heard dynamite. I suppose you blew the dam. If Claude. . . ."

Walt flared: "Shut up about Claude. I didn't blow the dam. I blew Kenyon's head gate into the ditch. We've got our water back, but I've an idea I've stirred up a hornet's nest as far as the rest of the country's concerned."

He thought he detected grudging approval in Jake's eyes. Then it was gone. Jake growled: "I don't see how the hell you managed to get us into this mess. If Claude had been around, Kenyon would never have got his hands on our water."

104

Walt said wearily: "Claude isn't around. Claude's dead, remember? You hounded him last winter the way you're hounding me now. You hounded him until he went up on the mountain after those damned broomtails just to shut you up."

For an instant Jake's eyes were filled with pain. Then they turned hard as bits of stone. They swept over Walt and settled on Rose. Rose flinched at their impact, but didn't look away.

Jake's voice was barely audible. "She's the one to look to when you're blaming someone for Claude's dying. She didn't love him. She was willin' to marry him only to get her hooks into Ramrod. He found it out the day he went up after those horses. Claude didn't want to come back. He didn't give a damn. You can't tell me Claude would die in a blizzard. He spent half his life ridin' in blizzards."

Walt had been watching Jake. He was shocked by Jake's accusation, but he knew at last why Jake hated Rose. In spite of his desire not to, Walt glanced at Rose, unable to help himself.

Her face was colorless. There was an expression of intense pain in her eyes. She looked as though Jake had struck her. She saw Walt looking at her and flinched again. He opened his mouth to tell her he didn't believe Jake's accusation, but Jake cut him short. "She didn't waste no time marryin' you after Claude was gone, did she? By God, that ought to prove to you that she was only after Ramrod."

Walt said: "Jake, I know what's eating you. I know what's been eating you ever since Claude died. You blame yourself for sending him up there. Only it hurts to blame yourself, doesn't it? So you have to bring Rose into it. You've got to put the blame on her to ease your own conscience. Well, you can blame her all you damned please, but she isn't going to be here taking your abuse. She's going to town and stay with Irish."

He said the words and put into them all the conviction he could muster, yet a nagging doubt rode his thoughts. Rose had married him less than three months after Claude's death. Could she have loved Claude and done so? Could she truly love Walt himself? His doubt was like a fungus in his mind. He avoided her eyes, knowing it would show.

But Jake saw the doubt and laughed triumphantly. "Makes you think, doesn't it? Wake up, Walt. All she wants is Ramrod. That's all she's ever wanted. She couldn't marry you three months after Claude's death if she really loved him, could she? And if she didn't love him then, she was only marryin' him for the ranch. Now, by God, she an' Kenyon. . . ."

Walt's voice was an agonized shout. "Shut up, god damn it! Shut up! I won't listen to any more!"

"You still ain't ready to open your eyes, are you, Walt? Well, you better open them pretty damned soon or there's going to be another grave out there on the hill . . . yours. Kenyon's after you an' he'll sure as hell get you before he's through. Then him an' Rose and Irish McKeogh can have Ramrod. Why the hell do you suppose Kenyon kicked up that water business in the first place? Why do you suppose he's tryin' to kill you? He was courtin' Rose before either Claude or you began."

Until now, Rose had stood in shocked and unbelieving silence. Suddenly she was in front of Jake, trembling with fury. "Stop it! Stop lying to him! You're sick, and your mind is sick. You know the things you're saying aren't true, so tell him they aren't. Tell him!"

Walt had never seen her so. There was a kind of glory, almost a grandeur about her, as she faced Jake. Jake's eyes fell before her burning glare, and slowly the fury faded from her face. She began to shake with sobs.

Walt closed his eyes. He realized his fists were clenched so tightly they hurt. He opened them and rubbed his hands together. It was an effort to keep from shouting. He said: "I'll tell you the real reason he's trying to kill me, if you don't already know. He hates Ramrod and everything connected with it. Most of all, he hates you, because you were behind his old man's death." This was striking back, and Walt knew it was.

He stopped abruptly. Last time he'd mentioned the possibility of a fight between Jake and Olaf Kenyon, Jake had almost had another stroke.

Now, Jake showed no such signs. Walt took a breath and went on, trying to convince himself, he realized, as much as for any other reason: "Kenyon was married to Sonja, wasn't he? And up until the time he died and you had your stroke, the two of you were friends, weren't you? Otherwise you'd never have given him water." Walt went on desperately. "I figure you were in love with Sonja, and the two of you fought over her. How did Olaf die, Jake? Of a gunshot wound?"

"No! He fell and hit his head."

Walt said: "After you hit him?"

"No! We never fought!" Jake was sweating, his expression anguished.

Walt said: "Then it's just coincidence that Sonja left the country right afterward. That's stretching the hell out of coincidence, Jake."

Rose touched Walt's arms. "Let him alone."

He looked down at her. Her face was streaked with tears. He'd never seen a woman cry who could look beautiful when she was crying, but Rose did.

Walt looked back at Jake, hating him suddenly more than ever before because of the doubts Jake had planted in his mind. He said, wanting to hurt his father as Jake had hurt him: "I hope you were really in love with her, Jake. It would be a pretty dirty business if you weren't."

Jake's hands gripped the wheels of his wheelchair. They tightened, and jerked, and the chair whirled. Jake sent it spinning from the room without a backward glance.

Rose asked: "Did you have to say that to him, Walt?"

He looked at her. "How can you be sorry for him? Hasn't he hurt you enough?"

She tried to smile and failed. "Maybe I understand him, Walt. Maybe you don't."

"How could I? He's spent his life telling me how much better a man Claude was. He nags and belittles until I wonder if I do anything right. He hates you and he's never failed to show it. How can you possibly take his side?"

"I think he honestly loved Sonja. Perhaps the fight wasn't his fault, but he's had to live with an awful burden of guilt all these years. It's no wonder he's turned bitter." She turned away and took the last pan of cookies from the oven. She closed down the damper of the stove. Then she turned. "My things are packed, Walt."

He realized, looking at her, that she did not expect to return to Ramrod—ever. But he didn't let her know he knew. Instead, he said—"I'll get the buckboard hitched up."—and went out the door. He needed a bath and a shave and a change of clothes, but that would have to wait until he returned from town.

Chapter Ten

The buckboard team wasn't in the corral, so Walt caught up a gray gelding and led him to the barn. He put Claude's old saddle on the horse and cinched it down. He wiped the saddle off with a cloth, wondering that it didn't show more evidences of long exposure to the weather. Walt had been gone over a week last winter at the time Claude died, and he had supposed Claude's horse died with him. Maybe not, though. He'd have to ask Jake about that.

He led the horse out of the barn and mounted. Old Mac came to the door of the bunkhouse and peered at him. Walt rode over. He said: "There's water in the ditches, Mac."

Mac's face brightened. He picked up his shovel that was leaning against the bunkhouse wall. "I'll go set it for the night."

Walt said: "Set it, but don't fight with Kenyon over it. Understand? I don't want anyone hurt."

Mac nodded. He peered up at Walt. "Did you blow the head gate? I heard a blast up that way."

Walt nodded.

Mac said: "Looks like he can't shoot much better than he does anything else."

Walt remembered the closeness of some of Kenyon's bullets. He said: "Kenyon shoots well enough. Don't underestimate him."

Mac headed up the lane, and then cut into the field. Walt rode down to the creek, crossed it, and let himself into the horse pasture, leaving the gate down. The horses were bunched at the far end in the shade of a cottonwood, stamping and switching flies with their tails. Walt crossed the pasture at a gallop.

He glanced up toward Kenyon's place, but saw nothing move. He let his glance run down the road, wondering if Kenyon had headed for town. Probably he had. He'd waste no time informing Bryce as to what had happened. He'd probably try to swear out a warrant for Walt, but Walt doubted if he'd make it stick—unless Irish himself wanted Walt in jail for Walt's own safety. Walt scowled. Irish hadn't better try to serve any warrants.

Walt didn't see anyone on the road, but there was a faint cloud of dust down toward town where the road disappeared behind a jutting hill. He circled the horses and started them across the pasture, urging them through the gate. Walt dismounted, put up the gate, then remounted, following the horse herd and driving them into the corral.

He caught up the team of steel grays he'd broken a year ago to pull the buckboard and led them into the barn, where he harnessed them. After that, he hitched them to the buckboard and tied his saddle horse behind. He drove to the house and halted before the front door.

Rose had several grips already out on the porch. Walt loaded them in the back of the buckboard. Then he went into the house.

Jake sat in his wheelchair, looking morose. Walt thought he looked sick and shamed, but maybe it was only strain. He heard Rose's steps upon the stairs and spoke quickly to Jake: "I'll be back before midnight. If you want anything, Mac will be in the bunkhouse."

"I won't want anything."

Walt said: "Kenyon won't try anything tonight. You'll be safe enough."

110

Jake growled: "Worry about Kenyon if he comes around. Don't worry about me."

Rose came into the room from the hall. She glanced at Walt, then spoke to Jake. "I'm sorry for you, Mister Rand. And I'm sorry I bothered to deny the things you said."

He grunted at her sourly. Rose studied him briefly, then turned and went out the door. Walt followed. He had the odd, almost desperate feeling that he was taking Rose away for good.

She climbed lightly to the seat. He untied the buckboard, then mounted to the seat beside her and drove out of the yard. At the road, he scanned it, looking for fresh tracks. He saw some, made by a horse traveling fast, but could not be certain they belonged to Kenyon's horse.

In the west, the sun was shining below the plateau, an enlarged and brilliant ball of red gold. The sky above the rims was the color of copper. Heat lay in the valley, but with the sun down it was less oppressive. Glancing into the field, Walt saw old Mac already working a sizable stream of water.

Rose had been studying him and now she asked: "What do you want from me, Walt? What do you want me to do?"

"Stay in town with Irish until things get straightened out."

"Jake will never be different."

"No. I suppose not. But I don't want you here at Ramrod now. It isn't safe. Kenyon's crazy. No telling what he might do."

"You're trying not to believe the things your father said. Thank you for trying, Walt."

He didn't answer.

She said, her voice low: "It's something you have to come to terms with, Walt. I won't be coming back until you're sure."

Why did anger stir him so as she said that? He said: "Don't threaten me, Rose."

"I didn't mean it as a threat."

He looked at her. The brush that lined the road whipped past, creating a blur at the edge of his sight. He said, with more insight than he'd had since this thing began: "What's happening has been building up for a long time . . . with Kenyon . . . with you and me. I won't say it's not partly my fault, either. I've had a chip on my shoulder about Claude ever since I can remember. He was three years older than me, and consequently could always do things just a little better than I could. Jake rubbed it in and made me feel it more."

"Why do you call your father Jake? Why not Dad?"

Walt laughed, relieved but without humor. "That is funny, isn't it? We always called him Jake. At least, I think we did."

"Could that have begun fifteen years ago, when he had his stroke?"

"It could, although I think I remember calling him Jake even before that."

Rose said: "I hope your sons will never call you by your first name."

Walt couldn't imagine himself a father. He laughed uneasily, and changed the subject. "I was right about Olaf and Jake fighting. But they must have kept it mighty quiet, or I'd have heard something about it before now."

"They probably did keep it quiet. Nick would know about it, though."

Walt nodded. He asked, as much of himself as of her: "How can a man hate like that and hide it? I couldn't."

Rose replied thoughtfully: "Nick Kenyon is a strange man. There's something about him that makes you think

of . . . ," she halted uncertainly. "Walt, have you ever seen a wolf on a chain? I have. He lay there in the hot sun, panting. I can still remember the way he looked at me. It gives me the shivers when I think of it. It was as though he would have torn my throat out except for the chain. That's the impression I get from Kenyon . . . that he's a wolf on a chain. I'm afraid of him."

Walt looked at her and looked away, ashamed of his doubts. He said hastily: "I know just what you mean. Only I always thought of it as sullenness. I guess Kenyon's just been waiting for the chain to snap, and now it has."

She said: "Walt, be careful."

He couldn't doubt the sincere concern in her voice. Damn Jake anyway. Damn him for planting doubts. Walt said: "Kenyon won't do anything. He could have killed me up at the head gate and gotten away with it by saying he was only trying to scare me off. Now it's different. If he kills me, he'll hang and he knows it."

"But does he care? Maybe he's gone too far."

Walt had to admit the possibility. By blowing up the head gate, Walt had reversed their positions. Before, Kenyon had had possession of the water. Now Walt had it. So now it would be Kenyon who must go to court to prove ownership—or who must take the law into his own hands. He well might do it, Walt had to concede. He remembered Kenyon's crazy persistence up at the head gate. He remembered the look of almost fanatical hatred in Kenyon's eyes.

There were a number of things Kenyon might do. He might rely on the law and try to get an injunction nullifying Walt's recovery of the water. He might try to swear out a warrant for Walt's arrest. He might dynamite the dam in Wild Horse Creek, so that neither he nor Ramrod could have the water. He might try further to inflame the other, smaller ranchers against Walt and against Ramrod. Or he might go berserk all by himself and try to kill Walt, or Jake, or burn the house at Ramrod.

Strain was beginning to tell on Walt. His head ached. The eye that had swelled shut was opening again, but it still was painful as hell. His body ached from the bruises inflicted on it in the battle in Bryce's office early this morning.

In gray dusk light he passed the Guilfoile place and looked down toward the barn, experiencing again the vague hurt he had had earlier in the day when Tommy failed to return his wave. A bunch of deer was browsing the alfalfa in Guilfoile's field where last night the horses had been. They raised their heads to stare curiously at the passing buckboard.

Rose said: "I want you to know something before we get to Irish's house, Walt."

He looked at her curiously.

"Nick Kenyon began hanging around Irish's house before I was even sixteen." She looked Walt straight in the eye. The light was poor, but there was enough to show him the effort her admission required. She went on: "I've got to be honest with you and with myself. Maybe I agreed to marry Claude to get away from Nick. I don't know, Walt. I just don't know."

Walt wanted to ask—*Why did you marry me?*—but he couldn't. He was ashamed because the question rose unbidden in his mind. He was silent as the grays took the last turn and entered town.

It was nearly dark now. The plateau rims to north and east and west made thin lines of deep gray against the lighter gray of the evening sky. Cedar wood smoke from the town's cooking fires lay over it, thinly gray and pleasant to smell.

There were other smells—the smell of the stable corral in which manure lay two feet deep, the pollen smell of dry weeds, the smell of lumber from which the heat of day is ebbing. Someone, somewhere, must have been cutting a patch of hay today for the aroma of that, too, was in the air. Walt wondered bitterly why a man would bother. There wasn't any hay in the country over a foot high and it wasn't time to cut it, anyway. Perhaps the man just got tired of watching it burn in his field.

He wheeled the buckboard into Main, heading down it toward the clapboard railroad station and Irish's house so close beside it. Far down the valley the afternoon train wailed as it entered the cañon, and the sound was mournful as the cry of a dove.

There were a few men along Main and they stared at the buckboard furtively. It was then Walt felt it, like something you smelled, or heard, or sensed carried along the breeze. It was so tangible it made his nostrils flare and made the short hairs stir at the back of his neck. Rose shivered, although it was not cold, and moved almost imperceptibly closer to him.

There was violence here in the town tonight, violence compounded of hatred and fear. It was furtive now, as furtive as the men who stopped after Walt went past and gathered into little, whispering groups. But furtive or not, it was deadly as the curling lip and silent snarl of a lioness just before she leaps.

Meanwhile, the normal sounds of the town went on. A woman sharply scolded a crying teen-age girl. A boy's shrill voice echoed distantly and hollowly: "Ollyollyoxenfree!" A dog barked, and a freight wagon rolled noisily out from the depot and started up Main.

These sounds carried well in the still, hot air. They hung over the town like a pall of smoke, changing yet somehow always the same, giving the town its identity and character. Never before had Walt felt tangible menace in a place. Now, reluctant to believe his own senses, he scoffed at it in his mind. He looked ahead at Irish's house and saw Irish standing bareheaded on the walk before it, a stubby pipe dead in his hand.

Irish knew the town better than Walt, and Irish stood with his head cocked, as though listening to a sound, one he didn't know but would recognize as soon as his ears picked it up.

No longer did Walt doubt that Kenyon had preceded him. No. The word was here that Walt had blown up Kenyon's head gate with dynamite.

Irish recognized them in the faint gray light while they were yet a hundred yards away. Immediately, with a show of unconcern, he put his pipe in his mouth and cupped a match over its bowl. The smell of his pipe smoke came down the breeze, commonplace and friendly and somehow reassuring. Walt pulled to a stop before him.

Irish helped Rose down. "What are you doing in town?"

Her voice was defensive. "A visit, that's all. Aren't you glad to see me?"

Irish McKeogh stood looking at her, his own eyes level with hers. Then he glanced at Walt. There wasn't enough light for him to see Walt's face clearly, yet he studied it all the same, looking for something, and at last looking away. He said, his voice deep and rough: "So you blew the head gate and now Ramrod isn't safe for her." Walt was silent. Irish's voice, while still soft, held an edge of baffled irritation. "You've lit the fuse on a bigger charge than the one you used this afternoon. You know that, don't you? Kenyon and Bryce were here an hour ago to swear out a warrant for your arrest."

"On what charge?" Walt's voice was tight.

"Trespassing. Grand larceny. Wanton destruction of private property. Assault with intent to commit homicide. Hell, you pick it."

Walt grinned to himself. "You issue the warrant?"

"I should have."

"But you didn't?"

"No, I didn't!" Irish was almost yelling now. "Go on, take that rig to the stable. Then get back here. I want to talk to you and I'm damned if I want to do it out here on the street!"

Walt leaned around and handed him Rose's grips out of the back. Irish stuck one under each arm, holding another in each hand. He stamped into the house with Rose following along behind. A match flared and a lamp came to life. The door slammed.

Walt turned the team around. He drove up Main, resisting the almost overpowering impulse he had to keep swiveling his head around. He couldn't let them think they had him buffaloed.

Chapter Eleven

The livery stable was east along Main Street, about half a block beyond Massey's store. Vacant lots grown high with weeds separated the two, but in spite of the distance Massey complained a lot in winter about the smell of the wet and uncleaned corral behind the stable — at least whenever the wind was from the east. The stable was a huge, graying building of unpainted, rough-sawed boards that had shrunk after it was built, leaving cracks about a quarter inch wide. In winter, when a blizzard blew, being inside it was little better than being outside, and the coats of the stable horses were as heavy as though they wintered in the open.

The huge sliding door was open, so Walt drove the buckboard inside. There was a lantern hanging from a beam between the door and the tack room. Under the lantern lounged a group of men.

Half a dozen mothmillers flitted around the lantern, bumping it occasionally with an audible sound. Nels Jordan, the tall, thin stableman, straightened up from his hunkered position, came around, and took the reins from Walt.

Walt said: "Rose is staying with Irish for a few days. Keep the rig here until she wants it."

"Sure." Nels mounted to the seat, throwing a furtive glance at the group under the lantern. Walt untied his saddle horse from behind the rig, and Nels drove it back into the stable out of the way. Walt could hear the *clink* of tugs and singletrees as Nels unhitched.

Walt stood at the head of his horse, knowing he ought to mount and ride out, but held still by some obscure defiance. Two of the men under the lantern had participated in the beating he'd received earlier in Bryce's office. One was Hamp Richards, who was studying the ground at his feet with elaborate care. The other was burly, scowling Jess Armstrong.

Neither of the two was looking at Walt. But the others were. Walt could feel their hostility although their eyes were blank and coolly appraising, neither friendly nor pointedly unfriendly.

He had a rash impulse to take up this morning's quarrel again with Hamp Richards and Armstrong, and resisted it with difficulty. No use turning any more people against him. There were enough in that category already.

Yet it angered him to be so calculatingly appraised, for he thought he knew what was in their minds. Hamp and Jess Armstrong had been talking some kind of violence, some kind of retaliation against Walt and Ramrod. The others were not convinced, so they studied Walt, trying to decide in their own minds how effectively Walt would fight.

It was common knowledge that Ramrod's crew was on the mountain. It was also common knowledge that Jake was crippled and that Mac was old without the stomach for violence. They knew they had only Walt to contend with—and possibly Irish McKeogh.

Jess Armstrong must have felt the intensity of Walt's glance upon him, for he looked up and met Walt's eyes. In his face was a compulsion to do or say something. He had been talking violence and now would feel that the others were waiting for him to make a move.

He snarled: "Well, what the hell are you lookin' at?"

A sharp retort sprang to Walt's lips, but he clenched his jaws and held it back for he felt it again, that anger, almost hungry hostility. It wasn't only in Hamp and Jess that he felt it, either. It was in the whole crowd.

They fidgeted and came to their feet. They looked everywhere but directly at him. They were like a pack of dogs, hair bristling, teeth bared, pretending indifference in spite of the evidences of hostility.

It could break out here, Walt realized. This growling antagonism could flare up and become a snapping, snarling brawl. They were hot and surly and teetering on the raw brink of violence. All they needed was an excuse. He felt the weight of the holstered .45 at his waist. If trouble came, here in the stable, it would be killing trouble tonight. Walt would take no more beating like the one this morning.

It was this that decided him. He dropped his hotly angry glance from Armstrong and jammed a foot into the stirrup. He swung astride, knowing the moment of danger was past, knowing as well that he might have done the worst possible thing in failing to defy them. They could mistake his reluctance for fear, and then they'd be hot on his heels.

The murmur of their talk came to him as he rode away. No words were distinguishable, but the tone was there. They were jubilant. Out of the hesitant ones the hesitancy had gone. They had faced him and made him back away.

A strange feeling of depression came over Walt. What was it that turned reasonable men to unreasoning violence? And when it was finished, could they have anything in them but sickness over what they had done? He knew they couldn't. Yet he also knew there would be no stopping them.

He shook his head savagely. It hadn't gone this far in Warbow. When a mob was thirsty for blood, it usually hanged someone or flogged them to death before it was through. This bunch was only surly, and angry, and wanting to beat someone with their fists. There was a world of difference—but couldn't a mob like this one that was building in Warbow become a killing mob? Walt thought it could, and suddenly his body felt as though a chill had blown against it.

There was a light in Massey's store. Massey came to the door and peered through the glass as Walt rode past. Walt raised a hand to him, aware that Massey couldn't see him, but waving from habit. A light frown sat on Walt's brow. He reined in slightly, then slacked the reins and went on. He'd wanted, just then, to talk to John Massey. Massey was a pretty good citizen. He looked at things calmly and sensibly. Walt hadn't stopped because he'd known, suddenly, exactly what Massey would say.

Massey would have said: *I've never seen anything like it, but I've heard of it. They're whipping themselves up to a pitch. Maybe nothing will come of it, but then again, maybe it will. If you're smart, Walt, you'll ride out for a few days. Stay clear away from Ramrod. With you gone, maybe it'll just blow over.*

Yes, maybe it would blow over and, again, with Kenyon and Bryce egging them, maybe they'd burn Ramrod to the ground. Maybe they'd burn the few dry haystacks left over from last year. Maybe they'd kill Jake, because Jake sure as hell wouldn't sit idly by while they attacked his home.

Walt glanced up at Bryce's window as he went past the bank. There was a lamp burning in Bryce's office, which was odd because Bryce always quit at six o'clock. Through the flimsy curtains, Walt could see a crowd there in Bryce's office.

Across the street, in Sally Croft's restaurant, there were several men at the counter. They were all along the street, not walking, but lounging against the building walls, or squatting on their heels, smoking, talking some, but mostly silent.

Each of them, Walt supposed, was fighting a battle within himself. Some would no doubt grow tired of intemperate talk and wildly improbable boasts. Those that did would go home. But the others would surrender themselves to the mob hysteria. They'd surrender their consciences and become a part of the whole. Then they would become deadly and dangerous.

Sonja Zarlengo was standing in the doorway of Sonja's Place. She called to him, and he rode over to her and sat looking down. She said: "Walt, go on home, for heaven's sake. With you gone all they can do is talk, and talk gets tiresome after a while. Go on, Walt. Get out of town before it's too late."

Walt grinned tightly. "I'm going, Sonja, in a while. I've just got to see Irish for a few minutes."

Looking beyond her through the door, he could see that her place was as crowded as pay day on Saturday night. He rode on, and saw that the Horsehead was similarly crowded. Hell, every small rancher on Wild Horse, Rye, Schwartz, and Little Dry Creeks must be here in town tonight. They'd come to see a show. They'd stay to become actors in it, if Walt gave them the chance.

He reined his horse across the street toward McKeogh's small house. He tied the animal to the porch pillar and went in without knocking. He closed the door behind him with a feeling of relief. He could hear Irish and Rose talking out in the kitchen. But for a moment he stood still, his back to the door, thinking.

It was strange. Here, where everything was as familiar as his own room at Ramrod, violence and hatred seemed remote and hardly believable. It seemed impossible that the streets outside were crowded with men itching to do him violence. It seemed impossible they were aroused by small and unimportant things that were not even their concern.

Walt conceded that the smart thing would be for him to get out of town immediately. But he wouldn't leave the country, he wouldn't leave Ramrod undefended. If they intended to destroy Ramrod, they'd have to destroy him first.

Irish yelled from the kitchen: "That you, Walt?"

"Uhn-huh." Walt walked back to the kitchen. Rose was cooking something on the stove, and it was hot and close in the kitchen. Rose was perspiring, and it gave her face a faint but not unattractive shine. Irish had shaved, and the stubby pipe was clenched between his teeth. He looked up at Walt with ill-concealed anger. He got up, puffing furiously and leaving a wreath of smoke behind him. He spoke as he walked toward the parlor: "Come on, I want to talk to you."

Walt felt just a little like a small boy being escorted to the woodshed. He grinned at himself wryly.

In the parlor, Irish swung around and glared at Walt. "Why do you ask a man's advice if you don't intend to take it?"

Walt sat down and stretched out his booted feet. He looked up at Irish. "I don't recall asking your advice. I came to you because you were sheriff and I wanted to do things legally if possible."

Irish scowled. The sounds from the kitchen became muted, and Walt knew Rose was listening.

Irish bit down on his pipe stem so hard it broke. He took the pipe from his mouth and flung it to the floor disgustedly. He spat the broken pipe stem from his mouth. Then he stamped out the burning embers on the rug.

Walt had never seen him so furious. Irish made a visible

effort to control himself, but did not succeed. He began to pace back and forth across the room, and at last he said: "That was as stupid a damn' thing as you could have done . . . blowing Kenyon's head gate. What are you trying to do, bait the bunch of them into . . . ?" He stopped speaking.

Walt said: "Into what, Irish?"

"Never mind! Never mind!" Irish's great fists were clenched at his sides. Suddenly he whirled and struck the top of the table with one of them.

Walt stared at him. What the devil was biting Irish? You'd think. . . . Suddenly Walt remembered the way Irish had stood in the street, head cocked as though he were listening.

Irish sat down abruptly on a straight-backed chair. His eyes were tortured. He seemed to calm himself with a great effort, yet his hands trembled as they lay on his blocky knees. He said: "Ever see a mob in action, Walt? No, I guess you haven't. But I have. I've seen honest, decent men turn into wild animals so quick it scares you. It's a kind of craziness that comes over them . . . a blood lust. They're like a pack of sheep-killin' coyotes workin' through a flock. Ever see coyotes do that, Walt? Ever see the look that comes into their eyes? They enjoy it, but it's a dirty, ugly kind of picture, the pleasure that's found in killin'."

He stopped, as though overcome. Walt stared at him, confused. Why was Irish getting so worked up? Had Irish himself once been a member of a mob?

Irish stared at him, hard. His eyes roved over Walt, from his battered face to his booted feet, pausing and lingering on the belted, holstered gun at Walt's waist.

He changed the subject abruptly. "What's that thing for?"

Walt said with a shade of defiance: "Fists aren't enough

when you're up against six or eight men. They beat the livin' hell out of me this morning. They're not going to do it again."

"I could take it away from you. You know that, don't you?"

Walt's eyes narrowed imperceptibly. "Don't try it, Irish."

Irish snorted. "Christ! Hasn't anyone got any sense left?"

Rose called from the kitchen: "Supper's ready, you two. Come on and eat. Maybe it will improve your dispositions."

Irish got up. He waited for Walt to precede him, then followed along behind. Walt wondered if he'd try to snatch the .45 and wondered, too, what he'd do if Irish did try.

He sat down at the kitchen table, and speared a venison steak from the high-piled plate in its center. Irish sat down across from him and began to eat hungrily. The heat in the kitchen was terrible in spite of the open windows and door. From outside came a murmur of noise, the murmur of people on Main Street. It was not the same sound as that made by a Saturday-night crowd, perhaps because it contained no women's voices. Or perhaps for another reason.

Irish asked: "I don't suppose you'll listen to any advice. But maybe you'll tell me what you intend to do now."

Walt said: "Nothing. I'm going back to Ramrod tonight. I'm going to send Mac up on top for the crew. Then I'm going to sit still and wait. Maybe all this trouble will peter out into nothing. But if it doesn't, I'm going to be ready."

"What if Kenyon tries to replace his head gate?"

"I'll stop him."

Irish looked at him and sighed. "I ought to throw you into jail. I should've issued that warrant." But there was no conviction in Irish. He ate in gloomy silence until he had finished. Then he asked: "Suppose Kenyon gets an injunction? You going to defy the court?" His tone was hopeful now.

Walt said stubbornly: "That water belongs to Ramrod. You know it and everybody else in the country knows it . . . including Kenyon and Bryce. I'm going to keep it until the irrigation season is over, until we've got enough hay assured to winter our herd. After that, they can serve all the damned injunctions they want. They can fight it out all winter in the courts."

Irish said: "If they get their injunction, I'll serve it. You won't fight me, Walt. You're not that stupid."

Walt glanced at him nervously. "Maybe not, Irish. Maybe not. We'll have to wait until the time comes. Then we'll see."

Rose got up and stood with her hands on her hips. "Stop it. Stop it! How can you sit there and talk about fighting each other? Isn't there enough trouble without talking about that? Just because it's hot and dry doesn't mean they have to turn into animals." She stopped for breath, looking at Walt. "Irish is right, Walt. Your stubbornness is only going to make more trouble. Let Kenyon have the water. Then go to court and get it back. A dry summer isn't going to ruin Ramrod. Burying you will ruin it. Can't you see that?"

"Sure, I can see it. Only nobody's going to bury me."

Irish broke in. "I wish I was as god damn' sure as you are." He faced Walt with his earnest, worried gaze. "Damn it, Walt, I've seen this happen before. I've watched a mob born and I know every step they take along the way. I made the same mistake you're making. I didn't believe. I didn't realize how murderous, how cold-blooded, how vicious they could become." He shot a glance at Rose that was somewhat agonized, and this puzzled Walt. Did Irish's mob have anything to do with her?

Walt said gently: "When was that, Irish?"

Irish put his broad, stubby, powerful hands up and rubbed his face with them. There was thick, graying hair on their backs. He kneaded his eyes with his knuckles a few moments, the way a man will when his eyes are tired. Then he took his hands away and looked at Walt. "Never mind. It doesn't matter. What does matter is that I don't want to see it happen here. I'm asking you, Walt, don't stop Kenyon from replacing his head gate. Let him have the water."

Walt shook his head stubbornly. "What neither of you seems to understand is that there's more than water involved. The water is only an excuse. Hell, those men out there want to destroy Ramrod. They've made it some kind of crazy symbol in their minds. If they can't use this water business as an excuse, they'll find another. No, by hell, I won't give in to them."

He stood up. He looked at Rose, expecting to see some kind of approval in her, some understanding of the way he felt. He saw none. She showed him only coldness and harsh disapproval. Had he been less angry and more discerning, he might have seen the paralyzing fear that lay behind these things.

Nor did he hear it in the shrillness of her voice as she spoke. "You're a fool, Walt! A fool! Irish is right and you're wrong, but you're too darned pig-headed to see it."

Walt looked at her coldly. "Maybe I am. Maybe I am at that."

He turned and stalked through the parlor to the front door. He stopped at the door and called back a grudging: "Thanks for the supper, Irish!"

Then he went out into the hot, still night. He didn't hear Rose's crying in the house behind him because his thoughts were all on the menacing murmur of sound that rolled along the street.

Chapter Twelve

Irish's house sat back from the street about twenty feet. There had once been a lawn, but now it was dry and dead and grown up with weeds and alfalfa. There was a dirt path leading out to the plank walk. Walt untied his horse and led him across the walk into the street. The animal picked his way daintily across the boards, not liking their sound beneath his hoofs.

As though at a signal, the light went out in Bryce's office above the bank, and a moment later Walt heard boots pounding down the outside stairway. Uneasiness crawled up his spine. Was it possible that they had been watching for him? Was it possible that they had gone through all the preliminaries Irish claimed were necessary, and that they actually intended to kill him? It seemed incredible to Walt. They wouldn't go that far. They wanted only to work him over and scare the hell out of him. They wanted only to use him as a whipping boy for their own frustration and anger.

He glanced west, past the railroad station, and could see the twin track ribbons, given a translucence by the stars, stretching away into infinity. He could ride west, now, and circle when he was clear of the town. He could ride west and avoid whatever they had planned for him up there in the street. But they'd made him back away once and he was damned if he'd do it again. If he backed off now, they'd be out at Ramrod before the night was done. Besides, they'd probably posted guards out there somewhere, on the chance that he would back off.

No. His only possible route lay directly up Main Street to the corner, and then north to the Wild Horse Creek road. Both Kenyon and Bryce would be there in the street when he rode past. It would be dark, save for the little light thrown out from the two saloons and from Sally Croft's restaurant. A man like Kenyon could stand in the shadows and shoot a rifle, and, when the hubbub died down, who could say with certainty that Kenyon had fired the shot?

Walt had sometimes wondered, in his youth, how a man felt just before he rode into battle. Now he knew. He knew the crawling feeling in the pit of his stomach. He knew the coldness that was like a ball in his chest. He knew that his fear was as much that he might not act as he wished, as actual fear of dying.

He wondered briefly what Irish was doing. Was he still sitting there in the kitchen listening to the murmur of the crowd in the street, evaluating that murmur in terms of violence? And what if it changed when Walt was halfway up the street? Could Irish get there in time?

But Irish had thought it was safe for Walt to go home alone. Suddenly and decisively, Walt swung into his saddle. He loosened the revolver in its holster, remembering now that he had forgotten to replace the bullets fired up at Kenyon's. He shrugged. Too late to do it now, and, besides, the chances were he wouldn't need the gun except as a threat.

He gigged his horse out toward the middle of the street and rode along it at a walk, knowing that a gallop or run would make nervous trigger fingers more so.

A voice, familiar but not recognized by Walt, shouted— "There he is! There the bastard is!"—and immediately the murmur of noise in the street increased. It was an odd sound, like surf beating against a shore, like wind sighing through the pines. It was the voice of a mob, wordless because individual words were lost, but articulate all the same.

They moved out from the walks as though at a command. The doors of both saloons and of Sally Croft's restaurant swung open and men streamed out to join the throng. Not all were dangerous. Not all were a part of the whole. But they added their bodies to those already belonging to the mob, and closed the street in front of Walt.

Something close to panic touched him as he saw the last pathway through them close. With difficulty, he resisted the compulsion he felt to look around. Perhaps thirty feet was all that now separated him from their ranks. His horse continued to travel at a slow walk, although Walt could feel the animal's nervousness in his bunching muscles, in his arching neck. He could see it in the horse's laid-back ears.

Suddenly the mob was silent; a stillness lay over the street as though each man held his breath.

There, in the middle of the street, Walt saw Kenyon's big shape and Bryce's gaunt one. He saw Hamp Richards and Jess Armstrong, too, and these were the ones he watched closely.

Swinging his gaze, he saw Art Youra standing on the walk, a little apart from the others. Youra looked scared, and worried, and oddly ineffectual. There had been a core of courage in Youra this morning, or he could not have stopped the beating they were giving Walt. Yet now the man seemed overwhelmed by the magnitude of what was happening.

It seemed incredible to Walt that this was really happening. Did they intend to drag him from his horse? Would they beat him with their fists, or would they find a rope and hang him from a tree? A cold chill began to crawl down his spine. He wanted to wheel his horse and set his spurs. He wanted to gallop down the street and out of town and shoot any man that stood in his way.

Their continued silence became more menacing than bloodthirsty shouted threats. They just stood there, like wooden men, waiting until he reached their ranks.

Was it possible that they'd open up and let him through? He thought it was. In fact, the more he considered it, the more likely he thought it was that they would do just this—unless Kenyon, or Bryce, or Armstrong, or Richards made some hostile move.

Walt remembered Irish McKeogh's words: *You've lighted the fuse on a bigger charge than the one you used this afternoon.* Irish had been right, too.

Twenty feet now, and still the silence reigned, although there was some small noise of scuffling feet and nervous coughing. For the first time Walt noted that many of the men before him carried guns. Some were shotguns and some were rifles. A few wore revolvers belted around their waists.

Armstrong was one of these. He stood, spread-legged, scowling, directly in front of Walt. His hand was laid suggestively on the grip of his holstered .45.

Hamp Richards carried a double-barreled shotgun pointed at the ground. Walt studied him, remembering the way Hamp had behaved earlier that day in Bryce's office and subsequently in the hall after the fight had rolled out there. Hamp had gone a little crazy then, needing to get into the fight, needing to get in his few licks. Hamp would be a man to watch in the moments that were to come, for he carried the most dangerous weapon it was possible for him to have.

Just thinking of what a shotgun can do to a man at close range turned Walt cold. Then, suddenly and inexplicably, his anger began to rise. He straightened in his saddle and his head came up. He stared first at Kenyon, then at Bryce, and laid his full contempt and defiance on them with his glance. He looked at Armstrong mockingly and withered Hamp with a stare before which Hamp's glance fell guiltily away.

Ten feet, and already a few of those in his path were beginning to shift aside. Walt stared at them frostily and kept his horse at this steady walk straight toward them.

The narrowest of paths began to open, and there was a low sound of muttering from the entire crowd. *Now!* Walt thought. *Now, now's the time to plunge your horse on through!*

His heels twitched, preparatory to sinking his spurs, but caution restrained him. If he plunged through that line, a half a dozen men would begin to shoot at him. He had to play it slowly and calmly, and, if he got through that way, he'd be in the clear.

Someone shouted: "Don't let him through! Close up!"

One of those moving aside murmured resentfully: "Hell with that! He'll ride us down!"

"Oh, no, he won't!"

Walt recognized that voice and yanked his head around. He saw Armstrong, the words scarcely out of his mouth, drawing his .45 from its holster. He heard the *click* of the hammer coming back and the sound was as deadly as the *buzz* of a rattler. Walt looked at Armstrong's eyes and saw in them the will to kill.

Armstrong was standing a little to the left, perhaps seven or eight feet away. Walt cursed inwardly. A moment more and he'd have been through. Now Walt had no choice.

He rammed his spurs home and his startled horse leaped ahead. Hamp Richards flung up his shotgun and pulled both triggers. The gun belched orange flame and birdshot that sounded like a wind going past Walt's head. The recoil sat Hamp down as though he'd been slugged.

Walt's horse, terrified and confronted again by a solid wall of men, reared and tried to whirl in mid-air. Armstrong's gun flared, and Walt felt a burn like that of a hot iron scar across his ribs.

He heard Art Youra's high, frantic voice even over the noise of the crowd: "Killers! Lynchers! This is not the way!"

Walt's gun was in his hand. Hell, if he turned his back on them now, he was dead. He clubbed his horse between the ears with the gun barrel and the stunned animal dropped on all fours and stood there groggily. With him still, Walt could look around and see Armstrong, his revolver raised to eye level, sighting along its barrel. An instant more and that gun would flare. Frantically Walt swung his own gun and snapped a shot at Armstrong.

Before the concussion of sound died from his ears, he heard the monstrous bellow of Irish McKeogh down the street. He stared at Armstrong as his thumb drew back the hammer for a second shot.

Armstrong had taken an involuntary step backward. He still held his gun at eye level, but it was wavering and beginning to fall away. He brought up his other hand and gripped the gun butt with both of them, his face contorted with effort. Walt saw a stain begin to spread across the front of Armstrong's shirt. In this light it looked black instead of red.

A silence had fallen on the crowd again, the silence of shock, the stillness of men who are appalled at what their violence has brought. Irish had been right, Walt realized. They had not been ready for death, and had only intended to beat and maul him and then send him away.

They stared at Armstrong, whose gun was slowly coming

down as if it was too heavy for him to hold. Armstrong took another step back, as though to maintain balance. He staggered, and would have fallen but for a man who stepped in close and caught his arm. The man said insanely: "You all right, Jess? Come on, what you need is a drink."

In his tone was hope, the shamed hope of a child who has killed a pet in a burst of rage, who now is sorry and wishing that the moment of death had never happened at all.

Otherwise, there was no sound save for the pounding beat of Irish McKeogh's feet coming along the street. That sound waked Walt out of his own shocked stupor. He glanced down at the gun in his hand from whose muzzle a thin, acrid plume of smoke rose. He glanced at Armstrong, leaning so heavily on the man that supported him that he almost pulled him down. He saw Armstrong's knees begin to buckle and saw Armstrong's head begin to roll aside. The expression in Armstrong's eyes was one of surprise and disbelief.

Irish, who had been running, slowed to a walk. Walt looked at his blocky, heavy shape. He looked beyond Irish and saw Rose standing before the little house, her hand over her mouth as though to repress a scream. She began to run then, holding her skirts up so that she wouldn't trip.

His mind began to work again sluggishly. Irish would have to arrest him. It had been self-defense, but the crowd would never admit it. They wouldn't let Walt go. Irish would lock him in jail, and the mob would stir again. Their shock would pass, and anger rise. Armstrong would become a great, good man who had fought for the rights of all little helpless men. Walt would take on the likeness of evil in their minds until nothing was left but to destroy him.

Someone came running from the saloon with a lighted lamp. Its rays flickered along the street, making grotesque shadows on the walls of the buildings across the street. To Walt, it was all like some kind of nightmare, where men were the grotesque, dancing shadows and all that was real was terror.

Irish came up beside Armstrong and looked at him, then at the man who held him up. He said harshly: "He's dead. Why don't you let him down?"

The men in front of Walt shifted as some of them moved toward Armstrong for a better look. Walt touched his heels to his horse's sides. The animal was still groggy from Walt's blow, but he moved out at a walk, and no one seemed to notice his going.

Before Walt's eyes was an image of Armstrong's contorted face, Armstrong who he didn't hate and with whom he had always been on the best of terms. The image changed, and he saw the life dying in Armstrong's eyes. He shook his head savagely to clear the merciless image away. No one could deny a man the right to defend his life. Walt's hand went to his side, under his shirt, and he winced with pain. His shirt was soaked with blood, and his hand came away slick with it. He wiped it on his jeans.

Armstrong had fired first, and his shot had struck. He had carefully sighted for his second shot, his deliberate intention to kill. Walt had been justified in shooting back.

At the edge of town he lifted his horse to a run, although the animal was still wobbly on his legs and well might fall. But Walt suddenly didn't care. He was alone, more alone than he had ever been before in his life.

But he wouldn't be alone long. They'd follow him as soon as they recovered from their shock. Then Walt would die, as Armstrong had, only in a much less merciful way. He shuddered.

Chapter Thirteen

Gradually, as the horse ran, he steadied and began to settle down. The town was left behind and the velvet night closed in on Walt. Overhead, incredibly bright stars lighted the roadway ahead. Beside it, clumps of sage and greasewood raised in twisted shapes, tall as a man astride a horse.

The plateau slumbered ponderously all around him. On the cedar-covered benches below the rims, coyotes bickered volubly and endlessly over some fresh kill, and across the valley a lonely one raised his mournful howl.

There was lamplight in the window at the Guilfoile place, and at several others along the length of Wild Horse Creek. The road up Rye Creek had a bridge and lost itself like a pale ribbon in the towering sage of the valley floor.

Walt desperately fought the panic that crowded his mind. He had never killed before and it had shocked him more than it had shocked the men who witnessed it.

He rode on, the miles fading behind under his horse's hoofs. If only the past few hours could be wiped from the slate. If only he had not taken Rose to town. If only. . . .

He shook himself like a dog emerging from water. That was a useless and foolish way to think. The harm was done, and no amount of wishing would change it. Morally and legally Walt was in the clear. Armstrong had given him no choice at all—kill or be killed, and Walt had done the only thing he could, quickly, unthinkingly, as instinctively as an animal would.

He wondered what Rose was thinking. Had she absolved

him in her mind? Or was she blaming him because he
hadn't listened to her, because he had refused to surrender
the water to Kenyon? He realized that he didn't know for
sure how she would react, to this or to anything else. That
puzzled him. He'd been married to her for several months.
In that time any man ought to know his wife well enough so
that in time of crisis he could guess how her mind was going
to work.

Why didn't he know? He went back in his mind, trying
to decide that torturing question. He'd known Rose fairly
well, even before Claude became engaged to her. She'd
always been pleasant, and pretty, and a good dancer, so
he'd always danced with her at least once every time a
dance was held at the Odd Fellows Hall. But he hadn't
been in love with her.

Then Claude had become interested in her, courted her for
three short months, and brought home the jubilant news that
she'd agreed to marry him. Walt remembered now the way
Jake had reacted to the news—with surly, scowling silence. He
remembered the way Jake had changed afterward.

Jake had previously approved of Claude and of most of
the things Claude did. He seldom nagged his older son, although he'd always been at Walt. But when he learned that
Claude was bringing home a wife. . . . Walt frowned to himself, remembering suddenly how Jake had begun to nag and
badger Claude, continuing it until the day Claude died.
Why? Why had the thought of Claude's bringing home a
wife so upset him?

For no good reason, Walt put his hand down and rubbed
the pommel of the saddle he was riding, Claude's saddle.
He wondered again why it wasn't weathered and hard from
exposure. It had been almost a week before they found
Claude's body, a week of alternate blizzard and thaw. Walt

found it odd, too, that the horses Claude had gone after wouldn't have gnawed the leather of the saddle, for they'd been near starvation. Yet this saddle had an unmarked sheen, as though Claude had just dismounted from it.

When you came to think of it, that whole business was odd. Claude had found the horses and started them down, but he hadn't gotten over a mile. Why? Could it be that his horse had got away from him? Could the horse have come in alone, leaving Claude to die, unable to catch up any of the wild broomtails he was driving when afoot? Walt was certain Claude hadn't been thrown. His body had borne no bruises, and he'd had no broken bones.

Walt shrugged and put the matter from his thoughts. After all, what difference did it make? By morning, he'd be forted up in the house at Ramrod, fighting off a mob. Chances were he wouldn't get out of the house alive. He'd never see Rose again, but it was comforting to him to know that she'd get Ramrod, or what was left of it, because Jake had deeded half of it to Claude shortly after he had his stroke, and Claude, in turn, had willed it to Walt.

How long would the mob wait? Walt's face twisted. No longer than morning. They had something now they hadn't had before—a reason. Walt had done something at last that gave them an excuse. Not an excuse for beating him this time, either—an excuse for hanging. His mouth hardened in the darkness. They could forget about hanging him, because they'd never take him alive.

He glanced up at the sky. From the position of the Big Dipper, he judged it was no later than ten o'clock. So he had several hours, four or five at least. Not enough time to summon the Ramrod crew from the cow camp up on the mountain, but enough time to send them word. Maybe they wouldn't come. Maybe their loyalty wasn't deep enough to risk their necks for Walt. But then, again, maybe it was. Oddly enough, now that the lines of conflict were clearly drawn, Walt felt relieved. He knew what to expect of the mob in town.

He rode through the gate and down toward the house. There was a light in the bunkhouse, but none in the house. He unsaddled and turned all of the horses but one out to pasture. Then he strode across the yard to the bunkhouse. He went in without knocking.

Mac, fully dressed, was lying in his bunk, reading. He looked inquiringly at Walt.

Walt sat down at the bunkhouse table and absently trimmed the wick of the lamp, which was smoking. He looked at Mac.

"I just killed Jess Armstrong, Mac."

He was grateful for Mac's failure to question him. Mac sat up in the bunk and laid his book aside. "You want the crew?"

"Uhn-huh. There'll be trouble before morning. It was self-defense, but that won't make any difference. They'll be here as soon as they can get organized."

Mac grunted. "Too bad you didn't get Kenyon an' Bryce, too."

Walt grinned at him. "Thanks, Mac." This was the first unquestioning approval Walt had gotten from anyone. It was as though Mac had said: *Boy, I know you. If you're in trouble, it's sure as hell not because you've done anything wrong.*

Mac got to his feet and reached for his denim jacket. He shrugged into it and crammed his battered hat down on his head. "You leave a horse in for me?"

Walt nodded, and Mac went out. Walt followed and watched until Mac had saddled and ridden out of the yard. Then he went toward the house.

He was quiet going up on the porch, quiet going in the

door. He needn't have bothered. He heard the steel tires of Jake's wheelchair as he closed the door behind him. He fumbled for a match and thumbed it alight. He saw Jake in its light, and crossed the room to light a lamp. Then he turned to face his father.

"You still up?"

"That's a stupid question," Jake said peevishly. "Any fool can see I'm still up."

Walt asked: "Why?" He saw the .30-30 in Jake's hands.

Jake growled: "You're in a jam, ain't you?"

Walt nodded. "I just killed Jess Armstrong."

"What about?"

Walt grinned. "He took a shot at me." He pulled out his shirttail and peeled his shirt away from the wound in his side. It was stuck with dried blood and he gasped as it came loose. He moved to the lamp and peered at the wound. The bullet had grazed along his ribs, and two of them showed white and bare in the wound. In the rest of it, blood oozed slowly.

Jake persisted. "He shot first?"

"That's what I said, isn't it?"

"Irish after you?"

Walt shook his head. "There's a mob after me. I figure they'll be here before morning."

"And you're going to fight them off alone?"

Walt studied his father in the flickering lamplight. At last he said: "I'm not going to walk out there and help them put the noose over my head, if that's what you mean." He stared at his father, wishing the old man's face wasn't shadowed so much. He asked: "What's the rifle for? Were you figuring on trouble?"

"When you blew Kenyon's head gate, I knew it was comin'."

Walt said: "All right. Get it off your chest. If you're going to give me hell, let's get it over with."

"I'm not going to give you hell. Just wheel me to a window when the trouble starts."

For a few moments there was silence between them. Then Jake asked: "Where's that woman of yours? In town where it's safe?"

Walt felt anger stir for the first time. "I took her there." He looked around the room, conscious of how little chance he had. Two men couldn't defend Ramrod. Ten men couldn't defend it against a mob as big as the one they'd have to fight.

Maybe it would be better to run. At least, if he ran, he wouldn't be endangering Jake and the ranch. He said: "You and I can't hold this place. They'll burn it over our heads and you know it."

Jake shrugged.

Walt said: "You want me to go?"

"Scared? Yellow?" The old man's voice was harsh.

"I'm scared all right. But I wasn't thinking of my own hide."

Jake was silent for a few moments, looking at Walt's face. At last he said: "Don't worry about me. I've been half dead for fifteen years. We'll make it cost 'em to get that rope around your neck."

Walt nodded, experiencing again, surprisingly, the same warm feeling he had in talking to Mac.

Jake asked: "What's Irish McKeogh doing?"

Walt shrugged. "Trying to break up the mob, I suppose. Don't worry about Irish. He's not going to sit on his hunkers and let them do as they please."

Jake snorted. Then he said: "You send for the crew?"

"Uhn-huh. I sent Mac."

"Then all we got to do is wait. Go on out and make some coffee."

Walt went into the kitchen. He lighted the lamp there, then began to build up the fire. Rose's cookies were still spread out on the table where she'd left them to cool. Walt picked one up and bit into it.

Jake puzzled him. For the first time, he had heard approval in his father's voice. The chips were down, and, because they were, all the badgering irritability seemed to have gone out of Jake.

He lighted the fire and put the coffee pot on. Then he went back into the big living room. He heard a horse's hoofs in the lane, pounding toward the house, and tensed briefly until Jake's laconic voice spoke: "One horse. Relax."

Walt went to the door and stood beside it. As he waited, he punched empties out of his revolver and replaced them with live ammunition. He had just finished when he heard Irish McKeogh's great voice: "Hey! Walt! Are you in there?"

Walt opened the door, and Irish came striding in, scowling. He blustered: "You god-damn' fool, what did you have to kill Armstrong for? I can't hold that mob."

Walt peeled his shirt aside angrily. "What was I supposed to do, stand there while he used me for a target?"

"No. No, guess not. Sorry, Walt."

Walt asked: "Are they coming?"

Irish shook his head. He spoke contemptuously. "They're fortifying themselves with whiskey at Sonja's and the Whore's Head."

"Why didn't you make her close?"

Irish snorted. "She closed both places tighter than a drum. They broke in."

Jake interrupted caustically. "Why didn't you jail 'em, Irish?"

Irish flushed, but he looked at Jake unwaveringly. "You ever try to stop a mob, Jake? You ever really see one?"

"No, but I take it you have."

"You're damned right I have . . . back in Ellsworth, Kansas."

Walt looked back and forth from one to the other. Jake seemed to be baiting Irish, and Irish seemed to know it. Jake insisted: "And this is the same kind of a mob?"

"They will be when they get their bellies full of whiskey and talk. I know every step they take along the way."

Walt asked: "You expect them to come here?"

"Uhn-huh."

"When?"

"Daybreak, probably. I ain't making the same mistake I made last time. I ain't going to underestimate this mob."

Jake mocked: "Did you underestimate the last one, Irish?"

Walt didn't like Jake's tone. He said: "What are you two getting at? Is there something here I ought to know?"

Jake said: "Tell him, Irish."

Irish looked at Jake. "How did you find out? I thought nobody. . . ."

Jake chuckled nastily. "You don't think I'd let a woman marry into my family without knowing something about her, do you?"

Walt shouted furiously: "Damn it, what's going on?"

Irish said: "Don't get excited, boy. It's nothing about Rose. She was only a little girl at the time. But it might explain to you why I've bucked you so on this water deal. I was afraid of that bunch. I was afraid they'd do just what they're going to do."

Walt said with exaggerated patience: "It might explain a lot of things if you'd tell me what it is."

Irish said: "Yeah, I guess it would. We got nothin' left but time anyhow. You got any coffee?"

Irritated, Walt nodded. He knew there was no use trying to hurry Irish, so he headed for the kitchen.

He got three cups and the pot and carried them back into the living room. Irish said: "No cream?"

Walt grunted and returned for cream. As an afterthought he filled a plate with cookies.

Back in the living room he poured himself a cup of coffee, and sat sipping it while he waited for Irish to begin.

Irish seemed in no hurry. He sat sipping his scalding coffee, his forehead furrowed, his eyes full of pain. At last he said: "I should've backed you on that water deal, Walt. I could see that it was a steal. But they had me worried. For over two weeks I've been running from one end of the valley to the other, settling scraps . . . scraps over nothing, too. I knew there was trouble brewing. I knew they were looking for a goat. I figured, if you didn't stand still on that water steal, you were going to be the goat. They've got no love for Ramrod, anyway, because you've got so damn' much more than the rest of them."

Jake prodded. "Ellsworth, Irish. What about Ellsworth?"

Irish looked at him. "Rose will hate me when she knows. But you'd tell her, anyway, wouldn't you, Jake?"

Jake said: "I haven't told her so far, have I?"

Irish studied Jake, puzzlement plain on his face. At last he said: "Maybe I'll feel better with the damned thing out in the open." He looked at Walt. "Almost twenty years ago, I was married in Ellsworth. It was a wild town. The trail drives were still coming in, but most of that traffic had moved west with the railroad to Abilene and Dodge. Farmers were settling around Ellsworth.

"My brother, Rose's father, was one of the Texas

cowmen who'd come north with the herds. He saw the possibilities of settling in Kansas, so he settled there. In a few years he had control of over sixty thousand acres." Irish paused and grimaced ruefully.

"It was the same there as it is here. Some of the settlers didn't think it was right for one man to hold so much land. So they tried to move in on him. He backed up, holding what he could, giving up what he couldn't hold. They kept crowding, and the more he backed off, the more they crowded.

"It wound up the way it had to, I guess. Henry . . . my brother . . . was in town one night and a couple of drunk sodbusters set out to make heroes of themselves. They picked a quarrel with him, figurin' to kill him, I guess, because they had him boxed in a cross-fire. Only Henry killed one of them and the other lost his guts and ran.

"Feeling was pretty strong. The settlers demanded I lock Henry up to stand trial. I went along, figurin' at least nobody could dry-gulch him while he was in my jail."

Irish was silent now, his face oily with sweat. His eyes were tortured and he seemed to be hearing the sounds of that lynch mob again. He said: "There's a certain road they travel as they build themselves up to what they intend to do. The trouble was, I didn't know the signs. I figured it was just wild talk. I thought the days of lynching were past. I thought I knew those people."

His voice hardened. "I was wrong. They faked a gunfight in the alley back of the jail, knowing it would draw me out. And it did. But the minute I walked into that alley about twenty of 'em jumped me. Took my gun away and tied me up. I had to watch while they hanged Henry from a tree right beside the jail. When I got loose, I had to cut Henry down myself."

Irish raised pain-filled eyes and looked at Walt. "That's why I haven't backed you on this water deal. I've seen the signs of trouble in this country for weeks now. I've been busier this summer than ever before since I've been sheriff. Hell, everybody's been fighting, and I saw the signs. They were looking for a goat, and I knew you'd be it if you kicked up a fuss over that water. And I was right."

He finished the dregs of his coffee, and Walt refilled his cup. Walt asked: "What's the best thing to do now? You want me to leave?"

"That wouldn't help Jake, or me, or Ramrod. They'd burn the buildings and what few haystacks you've got left over from last year. They'd likely kill Jake and me doin' it. No, you stay here, Walt. By God, you haven't done anything wrong and I'm damned if I want you to run as though you had."

Walt said: "I sent Mac for the crew, but I doubt if he'll get back in time."

"Then there's nothin' to do but wait. Where do you keep your guns and ammunition? We'd just as well get ready."

Walt got up and led the way to the ranch office. He found three old rifles and a couple of shotguns that he and Claude had used when they were boys. He got his own new rifle and a wooden box full of assorted ammunition. He also found Claude's old .45, and Jake's Navy model Colt, a .36 caliber cap and ball.

They piled the guns on the table in the living room and loaded everything they had shells for. Jake's gun was loaded, but the loads were more than fifteen years old and it was doubtful if they would fire.

Jake watched them work with jaundiced eyes, at last saying caustically: "You know that's a lot of damn foolishness, don't you? There ain't a one of us that's goin' to see the sun set tomorrow."

Irish looked at him. "Don't be too sure, Jake. I'm not one that favors a lot of damned maudlin sentimentality about the members of a mob. If they come up here, they've engaged in attempted murder, and I'll treat 'em like murderers. To hell with this idea that they're upright citizens who are only misguided. When they start shootin' at me, they're going to be surprised as hell to find me shooting back, and I'll bet I'm a sight better shot than they are."

For a while after that they were silent, sitting around the single lamp, waiting.

For Walt, facing certain death was a new and highly unpleasant experience, but he was surprised to discover that he was not afraid to die. Rather it was the manner of dying which he feared. A bullet wouldn't be so bad. But hanging. . . . He shook his head, a bitter taste in his mouth.

Chapter Fourteen

The hours of darkness passed slowly in spite of the fact that they were already half gone. There was little talk in Ramrod's big, paneled living room. Each man was occupied with his own thoughts, his own private contemplation of death. None had any real hope of defeating the mob, nor did they delude themselves that the mob's anger would peter out. To each in his turn occurred the single way he could save his life, and each rejected it. Not one of them would run. So they waited, and occasionally talked, and kept their eyes on the windows that would soon turn gray with coming dawn.

Once Irish said, looking at Walt: "Kenyon's mad isn't all on account of Rose, Walt. It couldn't be. You know of any other reason he'd want to stir up trouble?"

For a moment Walt was silent. He looked at Jake, thinking of the argument they'd had earlier that day, but he didn't say anything. Whatever had happened between Jake and Olaf Kenyon was Jake's secret. If Olaf had died as a result of the fight, his death must have been accidental. Yet Walt knew that Nick Kenyon must have hated Jake all these years, blaming him for his father's death. He was surprised when Jake replied.

He said: "I know what you're thinking, Walt. You're thinking that Olaf and I fought over Sonja. Well, you're right. We did fight. We fought like a couple of wild animals. Kenyon fell over the cutbank into the creek. He hit his head on a rock when he fell. I went down and picked him up. I carried him up to the house, thinking I'd killed him. I ran all the way, with him in my arms. I got him to the house, and then I left. Walking home, I had my stroke."

"Kenyon died?"

"He never regained consciousness."

"And Sonja left after he died?"

Jake nodded. "I guess she blamed herself. But she had nothing to blame herself for. There wasn't anything wrong between us." The old man's voice was softer than Walt ever remembered. The harsh lines in his face had relaxed and his eyes were less bitter.

Walt asked softly: "Was Sonja in love with you?"

Jake nodded again. "But she was loyal. She'd made a bargain with Olaf and she wouldn't break it. I couldn't make her break it. I guess I got bitter. I brooded about it for a month before I went and braced Olaf."

Walt said: "If she was so damned much in love with you, why didn't she come to you when she heard you'd had a stroke?"

"She never heard. She left the country not knowing."

It was a strange, bitter story, but one that gave Walt more understanding of his father than he'd had before. It gave him, too, a better understanding of Nick Kenyon. Nick undoubtedly had carried hatred for Jake these many years, suppressed within himself because there was no way he could hurt Jake. His hatred had been increased by his losing Rose to Claude, and further increased when she married Walt after Claude's death.

Walt asked suddenly: "Jake, who found Claude's horse last winter? Kenyon blew a hole in my saddle and I've been riding Claude's. I was noticing that it didn't look as though it had been lying out in the weather."

Jake looked at him strangely. "Kenyon brought Claude's horse in the day after Claude left to go after the horses. It was what started us searching. We figured, if he'd lost his horse, he was in trouble."

"Where did Nick say he found the horse?"

"Wandering along the road."

Walt didn't say anything at once, although Jake and Irish both were staring oddly at him. He was thinking of Kenyon, who hated Jake and Ramrod with vicious intensity because of his father's death. He was thinking that Kenyon had wanted Rose and had known that he was losing her to Claude. Had Kenyon, seeing Claude ride out that day last winter, followed him? Wasn't it possible that Kenyon had somehow gotten Claude's horse away from him and then left him to die? Walt thought it was possible, even likely. He also knew it would be an impossible thing to prove, short of persuading Kenyon to confess, which he would never do. Walt could see the same suspicion dawning in the eyes of both Jake and Irish. He said finally: "We'd never prove it, Irish, not in a thousand years."

Irish shook his head. "I know it. But I'll bet he did it, just the same. I watched him hang around Rose ever since she was sixteen. I watched him chase away the others that tried to court her. He and Claude even had a fight over it, and I guess Claude won. Anyway, Kenyon quit trying to stop him from calling on her. But, my God, I didn't think he'd kill Claude over it."

Walt said: "We don't know that he did. We're only guessing."

Irish laughed bitterly. "Guessing, maybe. But guessing right. I'll bet he's been trying to figure a way to get rid of you, Walt, ever since you and Rose married. Some way or other, he hit on this water business. Maybe Bryce put him up to it. But all Kenyon wanted was to prod you into doing something like you did when you blew up his head gate.

That would give him a chance to kill you without getting hung for it."

Walt remembered the closeness of some of Kenyon's bullets there at the head gate. He remembered the almost frantic way Kenyon had fired shot after shot at him. Kenyon had obviously been trying desperately to kill Walt. When he had failed, he had gone to town and stirred up a mob. He may even have worked on Jess Armstrong until Armstrong was persuaded to fire at Walt tonight in the street.

It had been a shock for Walt to see the hatred in Kenyon's eyes last night in the saloon. It was an even greater shock to him now, to realize that the hatred had been in Kenyon all these months and years, festering and growing and becoming more virulent with each passing day. Already two men were dead, victims of Kenyon's hatred—Claude, and Jess Armstrong, who had allowed Kenyon to trap him into a gunfight with Walt. Nor was it over yet. More would die at dawn when the mob stormed up the valley to Ramrod.

Walt's thoughts returned to Sonja, wondering why she had returned to Warbow after all the years of being away. Perhaps she had heard, somehow, that Jake had had a stroke. Perhaps she only returned to be near him. But she'd never tried to see him, and Jake never went to town. Perhaps she had thought herself unworthy because of the life she'd led in the years she had been gone, and perhaps Jake, knowing she was in Warbow, had not gone to her because he was too proud to offer her only half a man.

Walt studied his father, whose face was free of bitterness for the first time since Walt's memory began. He asked: "Why did you fight so hard against Claude bringing Rose home, Jake? And why did you fight me so hard about the same thing?"

Jake looked at him, and then he looked away. He said quietly: "I didn't want a woman in the house. I thought I'd almost forgotten Sonja. I knew a woman in the house would remind me of her every day of my life. It did, too. Some ways, Rose is like Sonja used to be. That's why I was so god-damn' mean. I wanted her to go. I wanted to be able to forget."

There was shame in the old man's eyes. It embarrassed Walt because it was something he'd never seen in his father before. He changed the subject quickly. "I knew you ran Bryce off his range years ago. But how about the others? Are there any others in the valley that you ran off, too?"

Jake shook his head. "They all sold out, Bryce included. They sold at a loss because without range they didn't have much to sell. All of them but Bryce left the country. Bryce stayed in town. He got this water commissioner job. I'd supposed he'd forgotten what I did to him."

Irish said: "He hasn't. He's just been waiting for a chance."

Walt stared at the window. It seemed to him that it was turning a deep shade of gray. He got up and wandered outside. Looking up at the rim to eastward, he could see a thin line of gray in the sky. Dawn was coming then. He wondered where the men from town were now. Were they waiting out there in the darkness? Or were they still in town, preparing themselves to leave?

There was a faint chill in the air. A light breeze blew from the north, bringing with it the pungent smell of sage and spruce. Walt looked up at the sky. Stars were sprinkled liberally across it, sparkling like frost on the ground in wintertime. There wasn't a cloud to be seen, and Walt knew it would be another hot day.

Gradually the towering rims of the plateau took shape,

looming like gigantic gray walls. Walt put his glance on the place where the trail came off, aware that there was not yet light enough to see, but hopeful all the same. Perhaps he'd see the lift of dust there at the top of the trail. But he saw nothing. If the crew and Mac were coming, they had not yet reached the head of the trail.

He kept his eyes on the trail while the light increased, and at last turned his glance away. He knew he ought to get back inside. If Kenyon and Bryce and the mob were waiting out there, it was dangerous to stand on the porch. Yet he stayed, reluctant to go inside. He was thinking of Claude and trying to imagine how it had been that bitter day last November. Kenyon must have followed Claude without showing himself until Claude had found the horses. Then he'd probably hailed Claude and stopped to talk to him.

Walt had been on top of the plateau himself when a blizzard was howling. He knew how terrible it was for a man exposed up there. The sweep of wind struck with nothing to slow or break it for more than a hundred miles. He guessed that both Kenyon and Claude had dismounted and perhaps had stood behind the bodies of their horses to talk. He could imagine Kenyon seizing the reins of Claude's horse, mounting, and riding away. He could imagine how Claude must have shouted after him, how he must have cursed and screamed when he realized what Kenyon was doing.

A dull anger stirred in Walt's mind. Claude would have been unable to catch one of the bronchos he was driving, but he probably had exhausted himself trying. Then, he'd probably started for the ranch afoot. Somewhere he had lost himself in the swirling blanket of white. Even well-known landmarks changed when a blizzard howled around them.

Walt scowled and let his glance rove around the yard and outbuildings to the surrounding fields. How would they come, along the road, or skulking up the bottom of the creek? He guessed that they'd come up the creek bottom, for that way they could approach the house with little or no chance of discovery.

A rooster crowed from the chicken house down behind the barn. Walt started and turned to enter the house. As he turned, his eye caught movement on the road.

A buggy was coming up the road behind a galloping horse. It careened from side to side as it made the turn, straightened out, and a few moments later pulled to a halt at the gate. A woman got down and opened the gate, then got back and drove through. Without stopping to close the gate, she drove her buggy, again at a gallop, down the lane to the house. Walt ran out to meet her, sure it was Rose and was startled when he discovered that it was not.

Sonja Zarlengo jumped lightly down from the seat, flushed and as out of breath as though she had been running. She cast an almost frightened glance at the house, then turned and caught both of Walt's arms with her hands. "Walt, they're coming. You ought to be able to see them now down on the road."

Walt shook his head. "They won't come by the road." He looked at Sonja, thinking of her and Jake and Olaf Kenyon, thinking, too, that she had been too honest and loyal to go back on her bargain with Olaf. He said: "Go into the house. I'll put your horse up, and catch you a fresh one so you can get started back."

"Walt, I'm not going back." She looked at him fearfully, as though wondering if he would let her stay.

"We'll see. Now go on into the house."

"Walt, I can't. Not alone. Could I wait out here until you get back?"

He said: "Go on over to the bunkhouse." Without

moving the buggy, he unhitched her buggy horse and dropped the shafts. He made a rope hackamore for the horse and vaulted to his sweaty back. Then he rode over to the horse pasture and began to drive the horses back across the creek to the corral.

He knew the time was short. They might hit at any moment. A bullet could come slicing through the gray dawn light a minute from now. But he got the horses across and into the corral without incident. Sonja must have driven like a madwoman all the way from town, he thought, to outdistance the mob.

He caught up a fresh horse, and led him back across the yard to the buggy. He hitched up swiftly, and then tied the horse to a fence post.

Sonja came out of the bunkhouse and ran across the yard to him. The horse turned its head toward the creek bottom and nickered shrilly. Somewhere down there a horse answered, but the answering nicker was cut off short by, Walt knew, a hand clamped over its muzzle. He said: "They're here. Come on!"

She caught his hand and ran with him to the house. He flung open the door and pushed Sonja ahead of him into the house.

Irish glanced up at Sonja, then looked quickly at Jake. Jake looked at Sonja, seeming not to see Walt standing behind her.

For an instant there was something like anger in Jake's face. He looked away and smoothed the blanket over his knees as though to hide them. He said irritably: "Why'd you have to come here? Why'd you come? I didn't want you to see. . . ." He stopped, avoiding her eyes.

Sonja hadn't moved. She stood as though frozen just inside the door. Walt heard the buggy horse nicker again and pushed the door closed behind him. He knew the three of them ought to grab rifles and man the windows, yet still he didn't move.

Sonja's voice was a whisper. "Jake, I didn't know."

"I didn't think you did," he said sourly. "I didn't blame you." He looked up briefly and met her eyes. "I didn't kill Olaf. It was an accident. He fell off the cutbank into the creek and hit his head on a rock."

There was no relief in her voice, and no surprise. She said softly: "I never thought you killed him, Jake. I couldn't let myself think it."

"Then why'd you go away?"

She looked at him piteously. "I waited, Jake. I waited for almost a month. I thought you'd come. When you didn't, I thought you had changed your mind. I thought you didn't want me. No one told me you'd had a stroke, not even Nick, although I'm sure he knew. He blamed me for his father's death, and he blamed you. He made it plain he didn't want me to stay and he must have known I would if I'd known about you."

Jake grunted. "I wouldn't have wanted pity."

"And I wouldn't have given you pity. I had so much more than that to give you, Jake."

Jake said surlily: "You've been in Warbow for years. Why didn't you . . . ?"

She interrupted: "I'd been gone for years, too, Jake. I wasn't the girl you'd known." She stopped, her face flushing dully.

Walt coughed. He said: "They're here. Get down on the floor, Sonja. The rest of us had better get to the windows."

He snatched a rifle from the table. He went and crouched before the big front window. His eye caught movement out in the yard, then a voice raised in a hoarse, demanding shout: "Walt!"

Walt waited, hearing the tires of Jake's wheelchair as his father wheeled himself to a side window. At another window, Irish breathed evenly and quietly.

The shout raised again. "We know you're in there, you dirty damned killer! Come on out, or we'll burn the place to the ground!"

Chapter Fifteen

Irish spoke in an undertone: "Don't any of you answer 'em. It'll delay things a bit."

Walt crouched at his window, staying back far enough so that he could not be seen from the outside. His window faced southeast, so he was able to see the rims on both sides of the cañon. He saw the sun touch the rims on the western side of the valley, dyeing them a brilliant orange.

A plume of smoke raised like a pillar down in Ramrod's south hayfield, and Walt knew that someone had fired a haystack. Out in the yard, the men were staying out of sight. Once in a while Walt would see a flash of movement, but he never saw a fully exposed figure or a face.

Irish said contemptuously: "They're scared."

Anger burned like a steady flame in Walt, but he understood that this was as new to the men in the yard as it was to those in the house. Only Irish had seen it happen before.

They had to feel their way. They had broken into Sonja's two saloons last night and fortified themselves with whiskey. Chances were they hadn't eaten since supper last night. A few of them were drunk enough to be reckless, but the rest were uncertain, not knowing exactly what to do next.

Waiting and suspense would take care of their uncertainty in time. The effects of the whiskey they had consumed would wear off, and their headaches and nausea would turn them mean. As they grew more tired of waiting, they'd become more reckless, until in a body they came from their hiding places and stormed the house.

Outrage touched Walt. He could hear an argument going out in the yard behind the bunkhouse. It made him mad to realize that he was to be the victim of their bad temper, their hangovers, and their hunger.

The sounds of argument stopped, and for a while there was only silence. Then someone began to talk to them. Walt could hear the drone of the shouting voice, muffled by the walls of the house, by distance, and by the bunkhouse, until it was unrecognizable. Yet the inflammatory tone of it was plain enough. They were being egged on again, either by Bryce or by Kenyon, perhaps by both. They were probably being reminded of what a hard-working, honest man Armstrong had been.

Irish got up abruptly. "I'm going out and talk to them."

Jake rasped: "Don't be a fool!"

Irish looked at him. "They won't get me like they did in Ellsworth, if that's what you're worryin' about."

He went to the front door, and opened it. He went out onto the porch and stood there silently, waiting. The sun crept down the escarpment to the west and touched the valley floor. With it came the heat.

At last someone in the yard saw Irish and yelled: "Hey! There's Irish!"

Irish bawled: "Come on out of your holes, you goddamned yellowbellies! I want to talk to you."

They came out cautiously, in groups of two or three. Their faces were sullen and angry. At last they stood in a group before the bunkhouse. Inside the bunkhouse, Walt could hear someone systematically smashing furniture.

He heard the voice of Les Ordway: "Give us the murderin' bastard, Irish. Give him to us, or, by God, we'll take him away from you."

"He'll get a trial."

Walt's face twisted. *Trial be damned,* he thought. You don't try a man for defending his life. Yet he understood that Irish had to offer something.

Ordway sneered: "A trial! What kind of a trial, Irish? He's part of your own damned family. He'll buy himself a bunch of fancy lawyers and get off clean, with you helpin' him do it."

Irish's voice turned cold. "You can't have him, so get the hell out of here. I'll kill the first man that tries to get into the house."

There was no single answer that was distinguishable from the men in the yard, but the sound of their voices came to Walt, an ugly, menacing wave of sound. He looked at their faces, telling himself that he knew these men. But he didn't know them—not as they were today. Their eyes were cold and hard, their mouths grim lines in their faces. They were angry and had taken the step already that made them what they were. Before leaving town, they had committed themselves to hanging Walt.

A chill ran clammily along Walt's spine. He put up a hand and rubbed his neck as though he could already feel the rope around it.

In the yard someone bellowed: "To hell with all this talk! Let's get at it!"

A shot racketed out in the yard, flat and wicked. Walt flinched as it smashed through the window two feet over his head. A bit of glass struck his forehead and he could feel a warm trickle of blood from the cut. He wiped it away impatiently.

Irish stood on the porch, solid as a rock. He roared: "Come on, then, damn you! Who'll be the first?"

Walt stared at the crowd as though fascinated. There

was a pressure on those in the front to move ahead, but they pushed back against it and sullenly held their ground. There in the front he saw those who had beaten him yesterday morning in Bryce's office, Lucero, Hamp Richards, Ordway, but not Art Youra. Youra must have drawn the line at lynching. He saw Kenyon, too, and Bryce. He saw Dave Lynch, and half a dozen others he knew.

He lifted his glance to the rim, to the place where the trail came off, but he saw no dust. He tried to calculate in his mind how long ago Mac had left and how long it would take him to reach Ramrod's cow camp and return. Not yet. He wasn't due at the top of the trail yet with the crew. But Walt kept watching as though wishing for the sight of dust up there could make it appear.

He wondered briefly if the crew's arrival would make any difference. There must be twenty men out there in the yard. Could seven fight them off if it came to a fight? He doubted it.

Irish had stopped them in the yard, but he hadn't turned them back. They stood there sullenly, waiting him out. At last Irish knew he had lost and turned and tramped back into the house, slamming the door behind.

Walt asked: "Now what? They won't go, so what will they do?"

"They'll think it over," said Irish. "They'll smash a few things and maybe set fire to some of the buildings."

Kenyon and Bryce seemed to be conferring with Ordway and Hamp Richards. At last Kenyon turned and faced the house. He yelled: "Irish! We'll make a deal. Give us Walt and we'll give him a trial ourselves."

Irish chuckled bitterly. "I knew that was comin'."

Walt turned from the window and faced Irish, getting to his feet. He said: "Christ, Irish, this is crazy. I've got to do something. I can't just sit here and wait."

"You got no chance. That bunch out there is dealin' the hand."

"You seem to know everything they're going to do."

Irish's face showed no satisfaction.

"Isn't there a chance they'll give it up? Isn't there anything we can do?"

Irish shook his head.

Walt had to force himself to say the words: "Then I'm going out. What the hell's the sense of waiting? There's no help coming, and anyhow Mac and the crew wouldn't be able to do anything against twenty men. What's the sense of holding out until they burn the house and maybe kill you and Jake and Sonja?"

Something cold began to form in Walt's insides as he spoke. It was close now, that rope around his neck. Close and real. He thought of Rose and wished he'd said none of the things he'd said to her in the last two days. He wondered where she was and whether she was all right or not. It didn't matter right now why she'd promised to marry Claude, or why she'd married Walt. He knew he loved her more than anything else in the world. He wished he could tell her so.

Jake was looking at him strangely. Sonja had crept over near to Jake and was now crouching beside his wheelchair.

Outside, in full view of the house, the men were forming a court. Bryce selected twelve men to be on the jury and herded them over to one side. Bryce elected himself to be the judge, allowed Kenyon to be the prosecutor, and chose, of all people, Hamp Richards as defense attorney. The rest of the men stood to one side as spectators.

It was ridiculous. It was a farce. But it wasn't funny because it was deadly serious. Walt was reminded of a bunch of boys holding a mock trial.

With the window broken by that one angry shot, the sound of the trial came clearly into the room.

Walt said: "Well, Irish? Is there any point in waiting?"

Irish growled at him. "You try going out there and I'll slug you myself."

Bryce was making a speech to the men outside. "You all know the charges against Walt Rand. He's accused of the murder of Jess Armstrong." He looked at Kenyon. "Prosecutor, you got any witnesses?"

Kenyon staggered a little as he moved over beside Bryce. "Damn right, I got witnesses." He turned to the group that constituted the jury. "Ordway, tell 'em what you seen."

Ordway stepped out a little. "I seen Walt shoot Jess Armstrong dead."

"Armstrong have a gun?"

"Sure he had a gun. But he never drawed it until after Walt had shot him."

Walt breathed: "The god-damned liar!"

Kenyon shouted: "Anybody else see the shootin'?"

There was a murmur of assenting voices.

Bryce said: "Call some more of 'em, Nick."

Nick yelled: "Lucero, you see the shootin'?"

"Sure, I saw it."

"Was it like Ordway says?"

"Yeah. Armstrong never fired his gun until after Walt had shot him."

Kenyon called several more. Some of them staggered as they came out to testify. Walt saw a bottle being passed around among the so-called jury members. He could see the shine of sweat on the men's faces, could see sweat beginning to stain their shirts. He was sweating himself, but it wasn't from heat.

Irish said: "Walt, can we get out the back without being seen? They're all out front playin' at judge and jury. If we could get to town. . . ."

"What about Sonja and Jake?"

"They'll be all right. We'll lead the mob away."

Hope leaped in Walt. He said, already moving: "Anything's better than waiting. Let's go."

He started for the kitchen. He heard the tires of Jake's wheelchair, and Jake's voice called: "Walt!"

He swung around. Jake looked at him for a long moment, his mouth half open as though he were about to speak. But when he spoke, he only said: "Good luck, boy. Good luck."

Walt said: "Thanks, Jake. I'll be all right. Just be sure you don't do anything crazy."

Irish said softly from the doorway: "Come on. Is there a window that opens out on the back of the house? We'll be seen if we use the door."

"Uhn-huh. It's here in the pantry off the kitchen."

He pushed open the pantry door. The place was cool and smelled of apples and pickles. Shelves lined the walls and the shelves were piled high with all manner of canned goods. There was a small window at the far end.

Walt picked his way through the stuff piled on the floor, worked the catch, and pried it open. He fastened it up on the inside with a chain provided for that purpose.

Irish said impatiently: "Go on. Go on. Don't stand there all day."

Walt climbed up on a barrel and put his feet through the window. He forced himself through and dropped awkwardly to the ground. He glanced around quickly, his hand on the butt of his gun. He heard Irish struggling to get through the tiny window, and then heard Irish jump. The two of them began to run.

Chapter Sixteen

Behind the house there was about half an acre that Walt had plowed in the spring so that Rose could have a garden. He resisted his impulse to skirt it, and instead cut directly across it. He wondered at that. Here he was, running for his life, and he still hated to trample her growing vegetables.

Beyond the garden was the outhouse, and beyond that, by thirty or forty feet, the icehouse. Walt pulled up behind the icehouse and stopped, panting for breath. His wounded side throbbed from the hard run.

Irish halted beside him, also panting heavily.

Walt said: "Getting old, Irish?"

"I haven't run like that since I was a kid. Man gets older there ain't a hell of a lot worth runnin' for."

The smell of damp sawdust in the icehouse was in Walt's nostrils as he peered ahead through the screen of locusts and rabbit brush toward the creek. Faintly, back by the bunkhouse, he could hear voices as the mock trial progressed. His face twisted. The trial had, he knew, a purpose beyond that of convicting him. He was already convicted so far as the mob was concerned. The trial was a sop to their guilt, so that they had tried and convicted him and that, therefore, his execution was legal.

Walt heard the fidgeting of horses ahead at the same time Irish did. He said: "Over there. Do you suppose they had sense enough to leave someone on guard?"

Irish whispered: "I don't know. Suppose you circle up-country and I'll go down. If there's a guard, I'll talk to him and you come in behind him."

Walt nodded and slipped away upstream. He cut swiftly through the rough, brush-grown breaks that bordered the creek, and then began to work downstream. He was conscious of time slipping swiftly away. At any moment, he knew, the "court" might reach its decision and adjourn. If they discovered that Irish and Walt were gone. . . .

He hurried after that in spite of his determination not to. He came through the last screen of locusts and saw the horses that had been ridden by the members of the mob out on a little gravel flat beside the creek. A man was with them, and Walt recognized Nels Jordan, the stableman.

His eyes turned bitter. Nels had no stake in the water of Wild Horse Creek or any other creek. Nels had always been treated well by Ramrod. He must have come along, then, for the same reason people chase fire engines—for the excitement.

The sun was blinding against the white gravel of the flat. The heat of the sun was held here by the surrounding brush, unmoved by any vagrant breeze. A stench rose from the dried-up creek, a stench of drying green moss and dead fish, but there was enough moisture in the sand of the creekbed to make the air humid and almost unbearable.

Walt waited, his eyes searching the clearing for some sign of Irish. Then he saw the sheriff come out of the brush on its far side.

Nels saw the sheriff immediately and brought up the rifle he was carrying. Irish said nothing, but walked toward him unconcernedly. Nels lowered the rifle self-consciously, looking guilty. As the sheriff drew near, Nels looked around almost frantically, as though seeking support from some of those who had ridden with him.

Irish stopped a couple of feet from him and his big hand

swung. It struck the side of Nels's face with a loud, smacking noise. Walt heard Irish say contemptuously: "Open your mouth and I'll push your front teeth right down your throat."

Nels dropped his rifle and it clattered on the rocky ground. Irish called softly: "Come on, Walt. There's no fight in this one."

Walt crossed the clearing at a fast walk. The horses lifted their heads to stare at him. As he reached Irish, the sheriff said: "Turn around, Nels."

Nels looked at him worriedly, then swiveled his glance to Walt. Nels was wishing right now that he'd stayed in town. He turned around, though, and the sheriff brought his great fist down upon Nels's head like a maul. Nels slumped to the ground, unconscious.

Irish said: "Pick yourself a good horse, boy. We've got to stay ahead of them all the way to town."

Walt picked a big hammerhead gray. Irish chose a sorrel that looked capable of outdistancing anything in the bunch. Walt said: "Hadn't we better lead these horses off a ways? We need a little start."

Irish nodded. They went to work swiftly, tying the reins of one horse to the tail of another, until each of them had nine or ten horses in a string. Walt swung to the saddle just as Rose rode down into the creek bottom from the horse pasture on the far side of it. She carried a rifle across her saddle. Her face was dead white and her eyes were scared.

Irish said angrily: "What the hell are you doing here? I told you to stay in town!"

She looked at him with weary defiance. "I was up in a tree over there across the creek. I was going to shoot the man who tried to put a rope around Walt's neck."

Irish said irritably: "Well, go on back over there. When

they leave, go to the house and stay."

She shook her head stubbornly, her gaze unflinchingly on Irish's face.

Walt said: "Rose, you've got to do what Irish says. We're going to lead them off toward town."

Unspeaking, stubborn as a child, she shook her head. She looked at Walt, her eyes almost devouring him.

He said quickly: "All right, then, line out for town. Ride like hell and we'll catch you later."

She nodded, pulling her gaze from him with an effort. She disappeared down the creek, wisely walking her horse until she would be out of earshot of the house.

Irish said—"Come on."—and swung east out of the creekbed. Walt followed, his string of horses lining out behind.

They came out of the creek and the brush that lined it, and Irish dropped the wire gate that led into the big hayfield south of the house and buildings. He had scarcely ridden into it when a shout lifted over at the house, and a rifle bellowed.

Irish sank spurs into the sorrel's sides. Walt was right behind, staying to the right of the string of horses Irish was leading, hoping for protection from the bullets. He laid low on his horse's withers, spurring frantically.

Gunfire cracked over at the house like a string of firecrackers, almost obscuring the angry shouts of the men.

Walt flung a glance that way. The court had broken up, and the score of men who had composed it were running raggedly across the yard. They came to the fence, still firing carelessly and wildly, and started to climb through it. A couple of them got hung up in the fence on the barbs. In spite of himself, Walt had to grin.

Ahead of him, Irish had his string of horses at a gallop.

Walt yelled: "Bear right, Irish, or you'll miss the gate!"

Irish swung right. Walt glanced behind again. Most of the members of the mob were now across the fence, running toward them through the stunted hay in the field. One of them stumbled in a ditch and fell on his face.

But what Walt saw back at the fence made all humor disappear very suddenly from the scene. Kenyon stood motionless on the other side of the fence, rifle to his shoulder and steadied on a fence post. Even as Walt looked, powder smoke mushroomed from the muzzle.

The horse in Irish's string immediately beside Walt went down suddenly. The sound of bullet striking solid flesh was loud in Walt's ears even as the flat report reached them.

The horse, going down, yanked the one ahead of him to a halt. Walt marveled that neither bridle reins nor horse's tail had parted from the strain. The horse ahead of the dead one half squatted, then came up and kicked out viciously at the dead horse's head. Irish's arm was almost yanked out of its socket before he could let go the reins of the horse he was leading.

He bellowed: "Let 'em all go, Walt! Let's get the hell out of here!"

Walt released the reins of the horse he was leading and the whole string stopped. Walt dug his spurs into the gray's heaving sides, and the animal dug in and ran. Crouching low, Walt looked around in time to see Kenyon's rifle bloom again. Something like an angry bee buzzed past his head. Then Kenyon was climbing through the fence and running after the others.

The ditch at the upper end of the field was full of water that had flowed past the place Mac was irrigating and was now wasting itself somewhere in the big field southward. Irish's horse took the ditch like a bird, but Walt's fell short and his hind legs went into the ditch, flinging up a spray of water that drenched Walt's legs. The horse went to his knees, then scrambled frantically to his feet again, and went on.

Irish was down, dropping the gate. Walt rode through, and Irish put it up after him, to slow the pursuers.

They went on, and now Walt began to search the road ahead for Rose. He saw her at last just coming through a gate onto the road. She glanced behind, then drummed on her horse's sides with her heels and lifted him into a run toward town.

At the turn, Walt glanced behind. Already the pursuers had gotten the horses untangled, and about half of them had mounted and begun to race toward the road. The others were mounting, except for two, who had no horses, and these two were running toward Ramrod's corral. As they ran, a rifle spoke from the front window of the house and a bullet kicked up dust immediately in front of the running men. They halted, glanced at the house, then flung themselves belly-down on the ground.

Walt grinned sparingly. Jake was on the job.

Then Walt and Irish were around the turn and the view behind was obscured by a jutting shoulder of cedar-covered hill. Walt balanced himself lightly in the stirrups, leaning forward slightly to give the horse every advantage it was possible to give. Foam already flecked the horse's neck.

Rose was about a quarter mile ahead. Her horse was running hard and she kept turning to belabor his rump with the ends of the reins since she had no spurs.

Off to the right, now, in the south hayfield, Walt could see the blazing haystack that he'd noticed earlier. The outer layer of it had burned completely, which was what had sent up that first tall pillar of smoke. Now it was smoldering. It would probably burn for days unless a wind came up.

Just the sight of it made Walt angry, because the destruction of it was wanton and without point. There were probably fifteen or twenty tons in the stack, which would winter fifteen or twenty head of stock. Not a large amount but every little bit helped.

Walt could imagine how it had been set afire. The bunch had probably ridden past it, and someone, either wanting to show off or wanting to spite Ramrod, had flipped a lighted match at it. He hoped the pair who had been left at Ramrod by a shortage of horses wouldn't get any similar ideas about the buildings before they got away.

Behind him, the pursuers came thundering around the bend. A couple in front fired several useless shots at Walt and Irish, but the bullets came nowhere near. A man couldn't shoot accurately from the back of a running horse, and after the first burst the pair gave it up.

The sun was now well up in the eastern sky. It beat mercilessly against men and running horses. Rose's horse, running well ahead, raised a thin cloud of dust that drifted slowly off the road before Walt and Irish reached it.

Walt yelled: "Think we'll make it, Irish?"

Irish shook his head. "The horses won't . . . not at this speed. Somebody's got to slow down pretty soon or we'll all be walkin'."

But nobody did slow down, and the fleeing pair knew they could not be first.

The hectic happenings of the past two days now began to tell on Walt. His head felt light and his vision blurred. It was incredible to him that so much had happened in so short a time.

He glanced behind again. The pursuers had not managed to close the distance any. In fact, they seemed to be falling slowly behind, thanks to Walt's and Irish's careful selection of horses. Far back, Walt saw the pair who had been left behind crossing the field toward the road, riding two of Ramrod's horses. They'd made it to the corral, then, in spite of Jake and his rifle.

Walt saw something else, something that made raw fury flare in his brain. He saw a thin, bluish plume of smoke rising from the cluster of Ramrod's buildings.

Damn them! He wished now that Jake had killed the pair who were left behind. They hadn't had to set the buildings afire. Weren't they doing enough? Wasn't it enough to chase and hound a man, trying to kill him, without wantonly destroying everything he had?

There wasn't a chance that the fire would take a single building and nothing else. Before it was through, it would take every building on Ramrod, the house included.

Irish had seen the smoke, too, and he reined close to Walt's horse, reached out, and caught his horse's bridle. He yelled, over the sound of pounding hoofs: "What could you do? What do you think they'd let you do?"

Walt's eyes were tortured.

Irish yelled: "Jake an' Sonja will be all right. They'll get out."

Walt struck his hand away. He hauled his horse to a halt and whirled around, yanking out his gun. So great was his fury that he couldn't think. He only knew he was going to sit here in the middle of the road and kill as many of them as he could before they knocked him from his saddle.

Irish pulled in, too. "You damned fool, what do you think you're going to do?"

Walt didn't answer. He just looked at Irish. Up the road the pursuers saw them halted and howled with anticipation. Then, realizing that both Walt and Irish were armed, they pulled to a halt themselves. One of them got down to the road, knelt, and began to fire systematically at the pair with a rifle.

Irish bellowed: "You see? They won't even give you a fight. They'll stand back there and pick you off."

Walt had never been more furious than he was at this moment. He shoved his gun back into its holster and stood there, spread-legged on the road, clenching and unclenching his fists at his sides. A rifle bullet struck the road in front of him and showered him with dust and dirt.

Irish stepped up before him and struck him flat-handed on the side of the face. Irish's hand came back, and Walt got it backhanded on the other cheek.

He swung blindly, furiously, savagely, at Irish's face, but Irish ducked back, and he missed. He staggered forward, off balance. Irish caught his arm and deftly twirled him around, holding the arm high against his back. Irish gritted between his teeth: "You damn' fool! You stupid god-damn' fool! Are you going to stand here fighting with me until they kill us both?"

Walt shook his head. The edge of his fury was dulled, but the bulk of it still was there in his mind, burning like a glowing bed of coals. He said almost inaudibly: "All right, Irish. Let's go."

He mounted, and they rode out, still untouched by the rifle bullets being fired from up the road. Glancing back, Walt saw a thick column of black smoke rising from the buildings at Ramrod. As he watched, a tongue of flame leaped high.

He turned his head away. Somewhere, sometime, there was going to be a settlement for what those men had done today. Walt had to live until that day came.

Chapter Seventeen

The chase went on and on, the men of both sides riding grimly and silently in the blistering sunlight. Dust rose from the hoofs of Rose's horse, running ahead, and was thickened by that raised by Walt's and Irish's horses. They overtook Rose, and she rode with them, although her horse was now breathing with a rasping, ominous sound.

Walt's horse faltered and almost fell, but recovered and went on. Walt swung his head to look behind, squinting against the dust. He was in time to see one of the pursuers' horses go down, rolling head over heels before coming to a stop, lying on its side. The rider was thrown clear, and he got up immediately, limping noticeably.

The others swept on past, but they must have realized that the same thing would happen to them if they did not slow down. Accordingly they reined in their horses, dismounted, and lifted saddles and blankets off to air the horses' steaming backs.

Walt yelled: "Irish! Pull up!"

Irish looked back and judged the situation. He replied: "Later. Let's get out of rifle range first."

They went on for a few minutes more at a reduced pace. Then Irish pulled up and swung to the ground. Walt and Rose followed suit.

Walt said quickly: "Get your saddle off, honey. Quick."

He already had his own saddle off and was rubbing the horse vigorously with the sodden, rancid-smelling saddle blanket. When he had finished, sweat poured down the side of his face. It soaked his shirt and even his trouser legs. He began to fan the horse with the blanket. Rose had her saddle off and was rubbing down her own horse. She looked at Walt and gave him an uncertain smile.

The breathing of the horses, wheezing and hoarse, and the swishing of the saddle blankets were now the only sounds to be heard save for the ratchet sounds of grasshoppers out in the brush. Gradually the horses' breathing quieted. Walt kept glancing behind to where the pursuers were also resting their horses. He saw one saddle go back on and snatched his own from the ground. When he had cinched up, he went over and helped Rose. She clutched his shoulders, hard, as he tossed her up and her eyes clung to his face, although she said nothing.

Walt mounted. He said—"We'll hold our pace to theirs."—and moved out, with Irish beside him and Rose ahead of them.

The pillar of smoke at Ramrod had thinned now, but still it rose like a monstrous Indian signal smoke. Walt supposed that whatever building had been fired had caught completely by now, and this would explain the reduced amount of smoke. Soon, though, the fire would spread to other buildings and again the black pillars would rise.

His face was grave, streaked with sweat and dust. He raged and fought within himself, and the signs of the fight were plain in his eyes. But the miles flowed behind. The horses walked until they cooled, then trotted, then galloped, and finally ran again as their pursuers allowed eagerness to step up their pace.

One by one, they passed the small ranches, including the Guilfoile place, and then they were coming into Warbow, now at a dead run.

A bunch of dogs scattered from the road before them,

then converged behind them to follow, barking wildly, all the way to the jail.

The townspeople stopped what they were doing to stare at the fleeing trio. Walt pulled to a plunging halt before the jail building and flung himself from his horse. Irish followed suit while Walt helped Rose down, although she needed no help.

They didn't bother to tie the horses, but instead piled into the jail building and slammed the door behind them. Irish shot home the solid oak bar, and Walt hung a padlock in the hasp, then locked the door with the key which was in the lock.

Rose went over and sank dispiritedly into a chair. Walt mopped his streaming brow with a sodden sleeve, smearing the sweat and dust but not wiping it away. The inside of the jail was cooler by about ten degrees than the outside air, but later that would change. Later, when the sun had beaten upon its flat roof for a while, it would become hotter inside than it was out. It was a small building, perhaps thirty feet long and fifteen wide. It was divided by a partition made of steel bars in which there was a barred door. The rear two-thirds of the jail was given over to cells, of which there were five in all, each of them barely large enough to accommodate a cot. The concrete floor smelled of disinfectant.

They heard the sounds of their pursuers pulling up in the street outside through the narrow, barred windows set high in the walls.

Walt sank down on one of the straight-backed chairs at the front of the building and looked at Irish. "What now?"

"We wait."

"For what?"

Irish said: "Not a man in that bunch had a minute's sleep last night."

Walt said: "Neither did we."

"Then I suggest you get some now, if you can. Nothing's going to happen for a while. They'll storm around out there and yell at us until they're hoarse. But they're all packing hangovers and they're dead for sleep and food. They'll hunt themselves some food, some hair-of-the-dog, and some sleep in that order. Then they'll try and smoke us out."

Walt growled, glancing across the room at the gun rack and the ammunition boxes on the floor before them: "That's the time I'm waiting for."

Irish gave him a quick, sharp look. "So you've killed a man and acquired a taste for it. Is that it?"

Walt stared at him. "Irish, they've beaten and hounded me for two days. They've burned Ramrod. To hell with this turn the other cheek business. Someone's going to pay."

Irish stared at him sourly. "All right. Take it a little further. You kill half a dozen of them and then you get away. Do you think for a minute that your story's going to be believed? Warbow will swear that wasn't a lynch mob. They'll say, sure, they were mad. They wanted justice. They wanted you to hang. But they didn't intend to hang you themselves."

"What about Ramrod? How the hell are they going to explain that away?"

Irish smiled patiently. "An accident. A carelessly dropped cigarette. Certainly not deliberate arson. This is a peaceful gathering, not a mob, remember?"

"They can get away with that?"

"They can, and they will."

"You make it sound pretty hopeless."

Irish shrugged. "Face it, Walt. It *is* hopeless, unless we're prepared to kill a good many of those men outside. Figure it out for yourself. Which ones are you prepared to kill?"

Walt scowled. He said: "Kenyon and Bryce for a start."

Irish smiled grimly. "Look outside."

Walt stood on his toes and looked out one of the barred windows into the street. He could count about fifteen men, but he saw neither Bryce nor Kenyon. He banged into the cells at the rear of the jail and peered out the windows at the back and sides. Kenyon and Bryce were not in sight.

If they were there at all, they were either standing close to the jail, right against the walls where they couldn't be seen, or they were directing things from some other place of safety. Walt went back and sat down on a bench.

Irish said patiently: "Walt, they know how you feel. They know you're not a prisoner and that you've got your gun. Do you think they're fools?"

Walt didn't answer. He looked across at Rose. "What about her?"

"They won't hurt her. We can send her out any time."

Rose looked up, her eyes snapping. "You'll do no such thing."

Walt said: "Maybe something will happen. Maybe the townspeople. . . ."

Irish was shaking his head. "Don't count on that. They won't be able to get together on what they should do. And those that want to interfere won't have the guts to do it alone."

"You sound damned sure."

"I am sure. I've seen it happen before. I've watched the law-abiding townspeople allow it to happen because they didn't have the guts to interfere."

Walt looked at him closely, but Irish was looking at Rose. He seemed about to unburden himself to her, but Walt said quickly: "That wouldn't do any good and you know it, Irish. You go on back and get some sleep. I'll stay awake for a while."

Irish got up wearily. The sleepless night and the strain of both day and night had taken their toll of him. His face was haggard, his eyes bloodshot. He walked tiredly back into one of the cells and lay down on a bunk. The springs groaned with his weight. He closed his eyes and began to breathe heavily. In a matter of minutes he was snoring.

Rose looked at Walt. "I feel as though this was all my fault."

His voice was curt, more than he intended. "It isn't your fault. You had nothing to do with it. It's the heat and the drought. Maybe it's partly my fault. If I'd listened to Irish. . . . If I'd listened to John Massey. . . . But I wouldn't listen. . . ."

There should have been closeness between him and Rose, these last hours, and Walt knew it. Yet every time he looked at her he thought of Claude, and Kenyon, and wondered why she had been willing to marry so soon after Claude's death.

Outside, the shouting had died. Walt went over to the window again and saw several of the men straggling uptown toward Sally Croft's restaurant. Across the street on Irish McKeogh's porch sat two men, Lucero and Hamp Richards. Each held a rifle across his knees. The idea of flight occurred to Walt, but he discarded it at once, knowing that, even if he got away, they'd follow. They'd gone this far and they couldn't quit now.

Rose had been watching him in the same strange way she had looked at him earlier. Her voice was scarcely more than a whisper. "Walt, do you remember coming to town with your father one Christmas day when you were about eight?"

He frowned, trying to remember, trying to concentrate his troubled thoughts on what she was saying. Oddly enough, he did recall that day. He nodded. "Why?" But his thoughts had left her again and he didn't hear the words she said.

Her voice was soft. "It was the first time I'd ever seen you. I thought you were the handsomest boy in the world. I stood at the window for over an hour waiting for you to drive past on the way back home." Walt didn't answer. She said: "Walt." He looked at her.

For a moment there was hurt in her eyes, but it was replaced almost instantly by sympathy and understanding. She asked: "What are you thinking, Walt?"

"Trying to figure a way out of this damned mess. There's got to be a way. Hell, we can't just sit here and wait."

Irish seemed so sure that things would work exactly as he said they would. The members of the mob would rest and eat and drink some more. Then they'd be back and make a concerted effort to force the jail.

Walt tried to keep his thoughts away from whatever was going to happen when they finally did get their hands on him. But every once in a while memory of that ominous crowd in the street last night returned to his mind.

Irish had been right. A mob had a personality of its own, as different from the individual personalities of its members as night from day. Timid and uncertain at first, it became bolder and hungrier as the hours passed, as though knowing that inaction could kill it off.

Heat was building up inside the jail. Back in the cell, Irish tossed restlessly, his face shiny with perspiration. Walt looked over at Rose.

She puzzled him. There was fear in her face, and in her eyes. But it was not a frantic kind of fear. Rather it seemed to be a kind of uncertainty, as though she had not accepted the threat of the mob to hang him—as though she were sure it would not happen but was not yet sure how he was going to avoid it.

Walt frowned. He wished he could fully understand Rose, but there were too many things he didn't know about her, too many doubts had been raised. If he could only know what she was thinking now. She was watching him, unsmiling and serious, as though waiting confidently until he should come up with the solution.

He got up and began to pace back and forth on the concrete floor. Once he paused and stared out the window into the street. Hamp Richards and Vic Lucero still sat on the steps of Irish's porch across the street. Neither was talking. They just sat and stared moodily at the jail.

The town was quiet. None of the familiar sounds filled the air. There was no bustle of activity along Main, only a solitary woman, who scurried almost furtively out of a side street, entered John Massey's store, and shortly re-appeared with a small package under her arm. She scurried back into the same side street from which she had come, and the street was empty again.

Irish awoke and came from the cell where he had been sleeping, rubbing his eyes. He said: "Go on back and take a nap."

Walt didn't feel like sleeping. He was tired, but his nerves were drawn too tightly. He knew he'd never relax them enough to sleep. But rather than argue in the stifling heat of the tiny jail, he nodded and went back to lie down upon one of the cots.

He closed his eyes, lying on his back. He made his breathing become slow and even, but it did no good. His nerves screamed at him to be up and moving about.

In the front of the building, he could hear Irish and Rose talking in low, subdued tones. He caught the gist of the conversation through a word or phrase understood here and there. Irish was trying to persuade Rose to leave, and she was refusing stubbornly. At last, Irish gave up.

A few flies droned through the still and stifling air. Somewhere outside a hen cackled the news that she had produced an egg. A horse whinnied and a grasshopper flew through the barred window and landed on the floor.

Walt dozed. He didn't know how long, but he came awake suddenly and sat straight up on the cot. He was soaked with sweat. His eyes were wide, and his throat was closed as though he were choking.

The dream had been real as life: fire eating away at the jail door—a battering ram—then the men storming inside to seize Walt and drag him out. A rope around his neck—a horse bolting away from a vicious quirt—and then the choking that waked him up.

Irish was looking at him. "Nightmare?"

Walt grinned shakily and rolled. He kept rubbing his neck as though it hurt. Rose was watching him, too, and her eyes were bright with tears.

Chapter Eighteen

In mid-afternoon they began to appear in the streets again. They came by ones and twos from the places they had been, some from the saloons, some from Sally Croft's restaurant, some from the livery barn brushing hay from their clothes.

At first they were silent, almost subdued. They gathered in small groups to talk. And now, having heard nothing at all from the occupants of the jail, Kenyon and Bryce also appeared in the street.

Irish stared at them through the window, with Walt peering over his shoulder. Irish was so short that he had to stand on a chair, but Walt could see out by standing on his toes. Irish spoke over his shoulder. "They've got to whip themselves up again. Before they do, I'm going to try once more."

He turned and got down off the chair. He ran his fingers through his lion's mane of hair, and then crammed his hat over it.

He unbarred and unlocked the door, and stepped outside. Instantly Kenyon bellowed: "Decided to give him to us, Irish?"

Walt was peering through a crack in the door at Irish and saw the sheriff shake his head implacably. "I'll never give him to you. Go on home."

Again that menacing murmur arose, the murmur of many dissenting voices.

Irish bawled: "Go home, damn you, or they'll be more dead men than Walt Rand in Warbow tonight!"

Bryce yelled: "Irish, who the hell are you workin' for? Who put you in that job?"

"The people."

Bryce shouted: "We're the people! We put you in as sheriff. We've tried and convicted Walt Rand for the murder of Jess Armstrong. Now, by God, you turn him over to us. You think you're bigger than the will of the people?"

Irish laughed bitterly and without humor. There was a resigned weariness in his voice as he replied: "Would any one of you, in Walt's place, consider that a trial? No, sir, you can't have him. Try takin' him an' someone's going to get hurt. Bryce, you're going to be first. Try taking this jail and I'll kill you deader than hell. And Kenyon, you're second." He turned his back on their shouting voices and came back into the jail. He looked at Walt. "They make a man feel so damned helpless. They stand there and look at you, and yell at you, but they don't hear you and they don't think."

Outside someone yelled: "Let's get this over with! It's too damned hot to stand around in the sun all day."

Walt went over and peered out the window. He saw Kenyon dispatch three men over toward the railroad depot. A few moments later the three came back with their arms loaded with firewood. They disappeared from Walt's sight as they came close to the jail. Walt said: "They've brought a lot of firewood. You think they're stupid enough to try and burn the place?"

Irish shook his head. He unbarred the door and peeped out.

"No one out here, so they're not figuring on burning the door. And they can't burn the building."

"How about the roof?"

Irish shook his head. "It's tar and gravel. The gravel's

184

half an inch thick. No, I don't think they're figuring on that. I expect they're going to try and smoke us out. There's a light breeze blowing from the north."

Rose spoke now for the first time in quite a while. "Couldn't we send for help? I could go out and get off a wire. Help could come in on the train."

Irish shook his head. "They wouldn't let you near the telegraph office, for one thing. For another, there isn't time for help to come. Don't think it didn't occur to me last night."

Walt said: "There's no one we can ask for help, Rose, unless it would be the governor in Denver. And that's almost three hundred miles away."

A faint smell of smoke came drifting in from the window. It was narrow and there was no glass in it. The glass had been broken out long ago by boys with rocks and never replaced because the building was so seldom used.

Walt said: "We'd better see if we can't block off that window!" He went to the rear of the jail, looking around for something with which to close it off. There was nothing, except for the blankets on the bunks inside the cells.

He got a blanket and climbed on a bench before the window through which the smoke was coming. He started to stuff it into the window, but outside a gun barked and a bullet, striking the windowsill, showered him with splinters and dust.

He grabbed for his gun, dropping the blanket and angered beyond endurance. Irish's sharp voice said: "Walt!"

Walt looked around, then climbed resignedly down off the bench. Irish was right, of course. If he showed enough of himself at the window to be able to shoot, they'd riddle him with bullets.

Walt stood momentarily under the window. He could

see the thin blue smoke rising from the fire they'd built under it. Beyond that he could see the plateau and the headwaters of both Wild Horse and Rye Creeks. Again today puffy clouds hung up there on the horizon. The breeze stirred, bringing a cloud of smoke in through the window. It also brought in the heat of the fire.

Walt said: "The other windows. If we could block them off, there'd be no draft."

He picked up the blanket and headed for the front window. Irish snatched the blanket and flung it at the window. Immediately a rifle bellowed in the street. The blanket fell back. Irish said: "They've thought of that, too."

Walt's voice rose to a shout. "So what do we do? Damn it, what do we do?"

"We wait. Lie down on the floor. It'll be cooler there, and the smoke won't be so bad."

Rose, coughing from the smoke, was first to lie on the floor. Walt laid down beside her, wondering about her. She hadn't said much for a long time. He said: "Honey, go on out. There's no need for you to take this, and they won't hurt you."

She shook her head stubbornly.

Walt said: "We could force you to go. We could push you out the door."

She looked at him without speaking.

Walt shrugged and sighed. "All right. You win. But I don't see why. . . ."

He hardly heard her voice, it was so soft. "I love you, Walt. That's why." She might have said more, but a heavy cloud of smoke rolled across the floor and she began to cough. Her eyes watered and her coughing seemed endless. But at last she stopped, out of breath and pale.

Walt had been coughing, too. So had Irish. Outside,

Walt heard Kenyon's voice. "Come on, five or six of you. There's a telegraph pole lyin' over beside the depot. Let's get it and finish this."

This, then, was the end. Ten minutes. Twenty at most, depending on how vigorously the men in the street were willing to work at battering down the door.

Walt knew at last what he was going to do—what he had to do. He leaned over and kissed Rose on the mouth. She looked at him in surprise, then her arms went tightly around his neck. Irish turned his back. Rose clung almost desperately for a moment, then released him and looked into his face. There were tears in her eyes, and suddenly the doubt Walt had felt the last couple of days was gone. He need never have doubted her. He wanted to tell her this. He wanted to tell her that he loved her more than life itself. But he knew, if he tried, he was going to come apart. Already his throat was choked and tight.

The air was now unbearably hot. Rose began to cough again, uncontrollably. Walt got to his knees, caught a lungful of the smoky air, and began to cough himself. He lay back down, flat on the floor, and dragged the clearer air into his lungs until he stopped panting. There wouldn't be much time once it began. He'd have to move fast.

Outside the shouting increased, and it had an edge of triumph to it now it hadn't had before. Shortly thereafter, the butt end of the telegraph pole struck the door with a resounding *thump*. Walt looked at the door. It seemed solid as a rock now, but he knew it couldn't stay that way. Repeated blows would loosen it and tear out its hinges and lock, or shatter the heavy door itself.

He swung his head around and peered at the window through which the smoke still rolled. The way he was lying, he could see the sky above the plateau miles north of the town of Warbow. Something stirred in his mind, vaguely elusive, and went away before the urgency of the moment.

The battering ram struck the door again and again. It was vibrating with each blow now, although it was still solid and secure.

Irish said: "They'll never make it."

Walt didn't answer. He wondered what Irish was really thinking. It wasn't that they were safe, that the door would hold. Perhaps Irish had seen the desperation in Walt's eyes. Perhaps he was trying to hold Walt off, to reassure him.

Again and again the ram struck. The tone of the shouting in the street seemed to change, to grow more triumphant, more angry, with every blow. Walt thought: *Now. Now's the time.*

He pulled his bandanna from his pocket and tied it over his face. It was slightly damp with perspiration and might filter out some of the smoke—enough of the smoke to make possible what he intended to do.

He came to his feet, then, drawing his revolver and thumbing back the hammer. He said steadily: "Stay right where you are, Irish. Don't make a move."

Rose cried: "What are you going to do? Walt! No!"

She had half risen, but the smoke made her coughing commence again. Walt said: "Get back on the floor. Neither you nor Irish is going to stop me this time. Do you think I'm going to stay trapped in here until they come in after me? Hell, no. I'm not. I'm going out. I'm going to make them shoot me, at least."

Irish protested, eyeing the revolver in Walt's hand. "You don't need to do this for me or Rose. That bunch won't hurt us."

"They won't unless you shoot at them. But when they storm in here, anything can happen and you know it. Besides,

I'm not doing it any more for you than I am for me. You think I want to hang?"

Irish started to get up, but Walt's harsh voice stopped him. "You think I won't shoot you, Irish? You're wrong. Maybe I won't shoot to kill. But I'll put a hole in one of your legs. I'm not going to be stopped, so don't try."

Rose cried: "Walt! Please! For God's sake . . . !"

One of the door panels splintered. The top hinge was so loose that sunlight filtered like a knife between door and jamb.

Walt backed across the room and turned the lock in the door. The ram struck again, and he felt the door give and vibrate savagely against his back. He put his hand on the bar.

He'd open it between blows of the ram. Then he'd plunge out. He couldn't be sure where he'd shoot when he began to shoot. Maybe he'd try killing Kenyon or Bryce. Maybe he'd simply shoot close enough over their heads to make them kill him. The ram struck again, and Walt's hand tightened on the heavy oak bar.

It stuck. The door had given just enough to wedge it tight. He tugged harder, then stopped as the heavy ram struck again. Walt threw his whole strength against the bar.

It gave less than an inch. He'd never make it with the gun in his hand. He let the hammer down carefully with his thumb and shoved the gun into the belt of his pants. Behind him he heard Irish getting up. The ram struck again, and Walt heaved against the bar.

Then Irish struck him from behind, knocked him against the door. They went to the floor in a tangle of flying arms and legs. Irish's right forearm was clamped tightly around Walt's neck, choking him. Walt was jammed against the door, and he kept waiting for the ram to strike again. But it didn't. He thrust his legs against the door and skidded Irish back toward the center of the room.

His ears picked up a change in the yelling outside. There seemed to be a higher pitch to it, almost as though there were a woman or boy out there screaming their lungs out. Then the shouting stopped. Except for that one voice, which sounded like a boy's.

Irish, straining against Walt, gritted his teeth: "Something's happened."

Rose got to her feet and ran across the room. She climbed onto a chair and peered around the edge of the window jamb. She said: "It's Tommy Guilfoile. He's pointing north."

Walt swung his head and stared out the back window. He knew suddenly what the thing that had evaded him a while before had been. The clouds over the headwaters of Wild Horse Creek were no longer white. They were deep gray, and from their dark undersides a solid sheet of gray had dropped until it touched the plateau.

Suddenly he wanted to laugh. Cloudburst. Waterspout. There was enough rain there to turn both Wild Horse and Rye Creeks into muddy, raging torrents before nightfall. There was enough water there to keep them running for a week.

He and Irish released each other and climbed to their feet. Walt continued to stare out the back window, but Irish shambled across and helped Rose to her feet. His voice was sharp as he said: "Walt! Come here!"

Walt crossed to him. He stood on his toes and looked out the narrow window, feeling the warmth of Rose's body against him. The fire must have died down under the back window, for the smoke seemed to be less dense. Or maybe the wind had shifted and was blowing in the window before them, keeping it away from their faces.

The men in the street outside were looking at Tommy Guilfoile and beyond him at the storm in the north. Behind them, Kenyon and Bryce were yelling: "Come on! Come on! To hell with that. Get hold of that pole. A couple more blows will bust the door."

The men who had held the pole hefted it, then stood looking at each other, uncertainty in their expressions. A couple shifted their feet and scuffed the dust uncomfortably.

The faces outside still showed traces of their fear, their irritable need to strike out at something. There were still marks of the pressures of heat and drought. But now something new had come into their minds. They were thinking again of their homes, their ranches, their dried-out fields that could now have water spread across them. They were confused.

Walt was watching a mob come apart at the seams. He didn't realize it at first. When he did, the tension and strain, the intolerable tightness of his nerves relaxed all at once, leaving him weak and loose, leaving him with an almost hysterical desire to laugh. He controlled himself with a determined effort, but a nervous chuckle escaped him in spite of himself. He, who had been as good as dead, was alive again.

Wes Ordway was the first to break. He looked at the jail, then at Kenyon and Bryce. He said clearly: "To hell with you. In two hours there'll be water at my place. When it gets there, I'm goin' to be there, too."

Hamp Richards looked furtively at Kenyon and Bryce. Then he slipped away down the street himself toward where the horses were racked before the two saloons.

Kenyon screeched: "Wait! Come back here! Wait! You sons-of-bitches, we got a job to do!"

Lucero looked at him coldly, as though seeing him for the first time. "Maybe *you* got a job to do. I dunno. I think this job isn't ours at all. I think I been talked into somethin' we ought to have stayed the hell out of." He turned and stalked away, his back stiff with anger.

After that, it happened fast. Bryce and Kenyon shouted at them until they were hoarse and red of face. They followed halfway to the Horsehead. Then they stopped and stood helplessly, switching their glances from the departing men to the jail and back.

Irish jumped down off the chair and strode across toward the front door, snatching a shotgun from the rack as he went. He leaned the gun against the wall and heaved on the bar. He said: "I want that pair of bastards."

Walt strode over to help. The bar stuck tightly, and it took their combined efforts to force it back. The door sagged. Between them, they managed to get it swung aside.

The street was empty now. Walt and Irish plunged out into it in time to see the last of the valley ranchers riding around the turn off Main.

Kenyon and Bryce were gone. Not home, where the others had gone, either. They were here in town. Walt had the uneasy feeling that it wasn't finished yet.

Chapter Nineteen

For a few moments, Walt and Irish stood motionlessly, staring northward at the cloudburst over the headwaters of Wild Horse and Rye Creeks. The sun still beat down mercilessly in the street and the sky overhead was without a cloud.

Rose came from the jail, running, and threw herself into Walt's arms. She clung to him with a fierceness that startled him, and then, as though she had been holding this back for a long time, she began to cry. It was a wild and hysterical kind of weeping that wrenched Walt's heart. He hadn't known she was taking it so hard. With his arm around her waist, Walt walked her across the street to Irish's. Irish kept looking around with angry uneasiness, and Walt knew he was looking for Bryce and Kenyon.

Inside Irish's small house it was comparatively cool after the heat outside. They trooped through the parlor, which also served as Irish's office, having in addition to the parlor furniture a roll-top desk piled with papers and Wanted notices. They went through this room and back to the kitchen. Irish grabbed the water bucket and headed out to the pump in the yard for a fresh bucket of cold water.

Rose looked at Walt, and suddenly he seized her in his arms and lowered his mouth hungrily to hers. It was a long kiss, a searching one and one that made him wish they were alone in the house. He heard the pump squeaking out in the yard as Irish filled the bucket, and held Rose away from him, wanting to say this now before Irish returned.

He said: "Rose, I've been a damned fool."

The little smile that was so much a part of her was back at the corners of her mouth. But her eyes were grave. "You have. And a blind one, too. Didn't you know that I've loved you since I was six years old? Didn't you know that I only agreed to marry your brother because I'd given up hope of ever having you?"

"You never told me."

"I thought you knew when you asked me to marry you, and when I said I would."

Walt seized her again. Irish came in and set the bucket of water down with a deliberate racket. Walt came up for air, grinning, feeling good clear to his toes. "Don't be such an old woman, Irish. We're married."

"If you weren't, I'd take a shotgun to you," Irish grumbled. "Kissin' her like that."

Rose laughed happily. She went to the icebox and got lemons and ice and made a pitcher of lemonade, but she couldn't seem to keep her eyes off Walt.

Irish drank half a glass without stopping. He wiped his mouth with the hairy back of his hand. "Boy, that was as close as I ever want to get!"

Rose asked: "What are you going to do about Kenyon and Bryce?"

"Arrest 'em."

Walt asked: "On what charge?"

Irish shrugged. "I'll figure something out. Can't get 'em for burning Ramrod. But I'll think of something. Maybe I'll try and hang Claude's death on Kenyon."

Walt hadn't thought about Ramrod for several hours now. He wondered if anything was left there. If there wasn't—well, he'd have to rebuild it, that was all.

Rose said: "You both must be starved. I'll fix you something to eat if you'll go on out of here long enough to give me a chance."

Walt got up and started for the back door.

Irish said quickly: "Huh . . . uh . . . Walt. In here."

Walt followed him to the front of the house. Irish sank down in the swivel chair before his desk. He said: "Walt, I can see it now. I can see that I was responsible for that mob."

"How do you figure that?"

"I let 'em scare me. I kept thinking about Ellsworth, and I figured they couldn't be stopped. But they could have been stopped if I'd done what I should have done."

"And what would that have been?"

"Last night I should have kept you here. I should have gone out and formed a posse of townsmen. I should have broken that damned mob up by force, if necessary, and driven them out of town. I could have done it then. Oh, they'd have groused and cussed me, but they'd have gone. After you and Armstrong shot it out, it was too late."

He picked up a pipe and filled it. Walt rolled a cigarette from the sack and papers Irish tossed him. When Irish had fired up, he went on: "That was the difference between this mob and the one in Ellsworth. The one in Ellsworth already had something to go on. This one didn't."

Walt said: "It's over. Forget it."

Irish lowered his voice. "It ain't over, and you know it just as well as I do."

Walt was silent. He hadn't wanted to say anything about Kenyon and Bryce to Irish, because he hadn't been sure. He still wasn't sure. He said: "Maybe you're making trouble where there isn't any. Maybe they're finished."

"You don't believe that, and neither do I. Bryce and Kenyon both are packing hate for a dozen men. They know

I'm going to be after them. My guess is that they're going to skip the country. But not—" he lowered his voice even further—"until they've hung up your hide on the barn door."

A horse pounded down Main Street outside and came to a halt before Irish's house. Walt got up and went to the window, then threw open the door. The rider was old Mac, and he grinned from ear to ear when he saw Walt. Half a block up the street, Walt saw the other members of his crew, and they whooped when they saw him come out on the porch.

They dismounted, and pumped Walt's hand, all of them talking at once. One said: "We figured you could hold out until night, but, by God, Walt, we're glad you're all right!"

Walt asked: "The buildings all burned, didn't they? Is Jake all right? And Sonja?"

"Sure. Sure. They're all right. All you lost was the one bunkhouse and the barn. We saved the rest. We was all for ridin' in here right away, but Jake wouldn't let us. He said . . . 'Don't you worry about Walt. He's my son, ain't he? He's a Rand, ain't he? You just get busy an' see that everything he's got don't go up in smoke.' "

Walt grinned. Rose had come to the door and was watching him with pride in her eyes. He returned her glance, his hunger and his need plain. She flushed, but did not look away. Instead she said: "The food is ready. I don't know whether it's breakfast, dinner, or supper, but it's ready. Then I want to go home."

Walt said: "Come on, Mac . . . George . . . Hank . . . Orvie. Come on and eat."

But they shook their heads. "It's a drink we need more than food. We'll get that and ride on out. Wind might blow some of those embers alive again. Be a good thing to be there if it does."

Walt watched them go. He was thinking that he'd made most of this trouble he'd had all by himself. Or maybe he hadn't. Maybe it took something like this to clear the air all around.

He went inside and out to the kitchen and sat down to eat. He was hungry, and he ate ravenously. But Irish ate only lightly, a tiny, worried frown between his eyes.

He was thinking of Kenyon and Bryce, Walt knew, thinking of the hatred and frustration that must be consuming them now. Kenyon had killed once. He had killed Claude as surely as though he'd shot him. He wouldn't shrink from killing again.

Walt wasn't so sure about Bryce. Bryce was through as water commissioner for conspiring with Kenyon to present a fraudulent water claim and he would be blaming Walt and Jake and Ramrod because he was through. But Walt wasn't sure he'd kill over it.

When they had finished eating, Irish said: "I'm going out and prowl around."

Walt said: "I'll go with you."

"No, you won't. Not this time. You stay with your wife." There was a warning in Irish's eyes as he looked at Walt. Irish didn't want to worry Rose, yet.

So Walt stayed and helped Rose with the dishes. There were things to be said between them, but this was not the place.

When they were finished, she said: "I want to go home, Walt."

"So do I. As soon as Irish gets back."

Her eyes were grave. "It isn't over, is it, Walt?"

He tried to lie, but he couldn't. He shook his head. "Irish doesn't think it is. He's out right now, trying to find out what became of Kenyon and Bryce."

"Walt, please let Irish ride along with us when we go home."

He shook his head. "I won't hide from them, not even behind the sheriff."

The sun was setting over the western plateau when Irish returned. The distant cloudburst was over, and the dying sun stained the remnants of the towering rain clouds a brilliant orange-gold. A light wind still blew from the north, but now it had the smell of moisture and a life-giving coolness.

Irish came banging in the back door, sourly cursing the flies, which were sticky because of the moisture-laden air.

Walt said: "Well?"

"Not a sign of 'em. They're not in Bryce's office or at his house. Nobody in town has seen hide nor hair of 'em."

"But you know they're here."

Irish nodded worriedly. "I know they're here. And the very fact I can't find 'em tells me what they're planning to do. I'm going to ride with you, Walt. And I want you to send Rose ahead."

"I'll send Rose ahead, but I'll ride alone."

Rose broke in: "Oh, no, you won't." Her eyes were sparkling and her jaw firm. Walt grinned at Irish. "You raised her. How did you handle her when she got that look in her eye?"

Rose said: "Don't tease, Walt. I mean it."

The sun was clear down now, and the sky was turning a bright shade of violet against which the orange clouds in the north made a brilliant contrast. Walt said: "Come on, then."

Before going out the door, he checked his revolver for loads. He seated it lightly in its holster. Rose watched him worriedly.

Walt didn't think Rose would be in any danger or he'd not have agreed to let her accompany him. He knew Kenyon was in love with her. He was sure Kenyon would take no chances of hitting her by mistake. So Rose was safe enough. Walt intended to increase her safety by not riding too close to her.

Irish had three fresh horses waiting in back of the house. He said: "I found the ones we rode in on and took 'em to the stable."

"Nels Jordan there?"

Irish nodded, grinning. "A scared Nels Jordan. He kept asking me if I thought Ramrod would take their business away from him."

Rose was looking around with fright in her eyes.

Walt said: "All right. Let's go."

He wasn't afraid of either Kenyon or Bryce. He wasn't even afraid of the two of them together, but there was no use kidding himself. He was scared to death of the pair of them hidden somewhere along the route he must travel going home. Kenyon had killed Claude by taking his horse from him and leaving him to freeze. Kenyon was considerably more cornered and desperate now than he had been then, and Kenyon would not hesitate to shoot from ambush.

A spot between Walt's shoulder blades began to ache. It took all the will he possessed to keep from glancing around.

Chapter Twenty

Walt helped Rose into her saddle. Her face was white, her eyes dilated with fear. She clung to his hand with a frightened expression as though she could not let go. Walt mounted and looked at Irish on the ground.

Irish said: "Go on. Go on. You can keep me from riding with you, but you can't keep me from tagging along behind."

Walt nodded. There was a tightness building up in his chest. It was one thing to face a man, another to make yourself into a clay pigeon for him to shoot at. Yet Walt knew that, if he did not give Kenyon his chance today, he might then have to wait for months, wondering, waiting for Kenyon to strike. A kind of pleasurable anticipation was in him in spite of his unease because, when Kenyon shot, then immediately Walt would be free to retaliate.

Rose was still looking around, expecting the shot to come at any minute. Walt said: "Ride out, Rose. I'll be right behind."

"Walt, I'm scared."

He grinned. "So am I. But if we don't give Kenyon his chance today, he'll wait and take it later."

"Irish could put him in jail."

Walt shook his head. "Irish has got no case. Kenyon would be out in a week." Still she hesitated, and finally his voice turned stern: "Ride out, Rose, or stay. But don't wait any longer." He hated to use that tone on her but the light was fading fast. If the light wasn't good enough for Kenyon to shoot, it increased the danger to her.

She touched her horse's sides with her heels and moved out of Irish's back yard into the weed-grown lot that bordered it. Walt followed, ten feet behind, and holding that distance.

Rose looked small and somehow helpless in the saddle of the big livery stable horse she was riding. But her back was straight, her head high. Walt called softly: "Good girl."

The weeds crackled under their horses' hoofs. The boardwalk echoed hollowly as they crossed it. Walt listened intently but did not hear Irish cross it. He longed to look around, but didn't.

Every muscle, every nerve in his body was tight as a fiddle string. Without seeming to, he looked from the corners of his eyes at the buildings lining Main, with a view to selecting those most likely to hide Kenyon and Bryce.

The pair might not be in town at all. They might be out on the road, at any point between Warbow and Ramrod. But he doubted it. Both Kenyon and Bryce would have realized that Walt could scarcely leave town before sundown, and they'd know they had little chance in the dark.

Walt strained his ears but could not hear Irish behind him. Rose turned to look at him, her eyes wide and scared. Walt asked quickly, softly: "Irish behind us?"

"No. Walt, where is he? Where is he?" Her voice rose.

He said: "Take it easy. He's probably over to our right in the alley. But don't look. Don't look that way at all."

If Kenyon's first shot found its mark, Irish would be no help at all. There could be no help from anyone against that first bullet. It was something Walt had to chance.

It took forever to reach the Horsehead. It took another eternity to reach Sonja's Place. Walt glanced quickly toward each saloon as he passed, then looked away again.

Ahead now was Sally Croft's restaurant on the right, the

Stockmen's Bank over which Bryce had his office on the left. The intersection lay immediately beyond.

Rose rode her horse at a walk, and Walt held that pace. He couldn't see Irish McKeogh because of the stores that separated the street from the alley on the right. He supposed Irish was spurring up the alley and would shortly come into view at the intersection that lay ahead.

Although he didn't glance aside, Walt could tell from the color of the light that sunlight had faded from the towering pile of clouds to the north. The street had turned gray and from now on it would grow darker rapidly.

Past the intersection, John Massey came to the door of his store, hat on his head, coat over his arm. He turned and locked the door behind him, then paused to watch Walt and Rose riding in single file. Glancing the other way, Walt noticed that the shade in the bank door bearing the word **Closed** was pulled down. His eyes lifted to Bryce's window although he fought to keep them down. He saw nothing.

Nervousness was mounting in him until it was nearly intolerable. The horse beneath him must have sensed it, for he tried to take his head and run. But Walt rigidly held him in.

Now he was abreast of the outside stairway leading to the offices over the bank. With shocking suddenness the shot laid its flat, wicked cadences over the nearly silent town. Ahead of Walt, Rose's horse seemed to squat and then leap ahead into full gallop. Walt could see Rose hauling frantically on the reins.

His own horse had leaped ahead at almost the instant Rose's did. He had gone almost twenty feet before Walt realized the shot had possessed a muffled sound, as though shielded from his ears by a building. Then, immediately, he placed its direction. It had come from behind Sally Croft's restaurant, and must have been fired, not at

Walt but at Irish McKeogh.

Walt turned that way with another sound in his ears, that of breaking glass behind him. He hauled his horse around, and with his right hand drew and cocked the gun at his thigh.

The window in the bank door was broken; the shade was torn from it. Through it poked a rifle barrel, and, as Walt watched, the muzzle puffed orange fire and a cloud of smoke. He heard the bullet strike his horse, felt the horse begin to fall at almost the same instant. He flung a hasty shot at the bank window even as he jumped clear of the saddle.

Kenyon's rifle roared again, hastily triggered, and behind him Walt heard a string of revolver shots that could have come from no gun but Irish McKeogh's ancient .44. Something relaxed in him, hearing that, and he thereafter put his full attention on the bank door less than fifty feet from where he lay.

The fact that both shots had missed told him Kenyon was overeager and perhaps nervous as well. He shoved his revolver out ahead of him, steadying it with an elbow, and squeezed off a shot at the man crouched in the bank door. He missed the man, but he hit the unbroken part of the door glass over Kenyon's head. It *tinkled* as it shattered and dropped in pieces to the floor.

Sounds were coming to his ears now too fast to be sorted out. Behind Sally Croft's restaurant, Bryce's rifle barked again, followed almost immediately by two close-spaced shots from McKeogh's gun. John Massey yelled something indistinguishable, and following that Walt heard Rose scream. Then he heard the sounds of her horse's hoofs as she galloped toward him.

Damn it, why didn't she stay clear? He risked a quick glance toward her and saw her coming, already halfway through the intersection and riding hard.

Walt had intended trying to get behind his dead horse where he'd be able to exchange shots with Kenyon on relatively even terms. Now he couldn't. Rose would come riding between and might well catch a stray bullet as she did. There was one thing he could do and he did it without hesitation. He put his knuckles down into the dust and lunged to his feet. Running, weaving from side to side to throw off Kenyon's aim, he charged directly at the door of the bank.

He could see the blued muzzle of the rifle weaving from side to side, trying to track him. He heard Kenyon's almost hysterical voice, "Go back! Go back, or I'll kill Rose!"

He was up over the walk before the words sank in. He couldn't stop. Perhaps Kenyon was trying to hit Walt. Perhaps he had been swinging the muzzle of the rifle and trying to hit Rose. The rifle barked and the cloud of smoke from it billowed out directly into Walt's face.

He shot, governed by anger, and then he crashed into the bank door and dived on through. Glass raked his belly. He felt Kenyon bowled over by the impact, and realized at almost the same instant that Kenyon's last bullet had found its mark because his whole right leg was numb and without feeling. The pain in his left leg as it struck had been considerable.

He was rolling and trying to bring his gun to bear. He tried to remember how many times he had shot, but he couldn't seem to do it. It seemed as though he'd shot a dozen times, as though this had been going on, not ten seconds, but ten hours.

Kenyon howled: "Walt! Don't shoot! Nobody's hurt." He was over behind the partition that separated the tiled bank lobby from the offices in the rear. Walt himself had rolled behind a desk used by bank customers as a surface upon which to write.

Walt didn't answer immediately. He was doubled up, his

back to the wall, his knees in the air, trying to see if any un-fired cartridges remained in his gun.

Kenyon said hastily, almost hysterically: "I'll go to jail, Walt! I killed Claude. Irish can put me in jail for that. But don't shoot!"

Walt said wearily: "All right. Throw the rifle out."

The rifle *clattered* on the tile floor and slid halfway across it.

Walt said: "Now, come on out yourself."

The light was almost gone, particularly here in the bank. Walt saw the vague shape of Kenyon rising from behind the half partition. He started to rise himself. Then, too late, he saw the revolver in Kenyon's hand. He heard its hammer *click* as Kenyon thumbed it back.

Maybe Walt's gun was empty. If it was, he was dead. He raised it with frantic haste to eye level and discovered he couldn't see the sights. Kenyon's gun flashed, its concussion deafening in this enclosed space, at this point-blank range. In its flash, Walt saw his sights. He fired instantly, with Kenyon's chest directly over his gun barrel.

Then he was being driven back and turned around by the force of Kenyon's slug as it took him in the shoulder. He was flat on his back on the tile floor without having any remembrance of striking it. Irish McKeogh's bull voice was roaring just outside the door. Kenyon was kicking the wooden partition behind which he had fallen.

Irish rushed in, gun in hand. Rose was right behind him. Behind Rose came John Massey with a lighted lantern.

Walt said: "He's behind that partition, Irish."

Irish seized the lantern from Massey and, with his gun ready, walked over to the partition. The kicking had stopped. Irish stepped through the gate and toed Kenyon's body. He turned, then, and said: "He's dead. So's Bryce. How're you, Walt? You get hit?"

Walt, lying on his back, saw the jagged hole in the plaster overhead. He said: "There's how he got into the bank, Irish. He cut a hole in the floor and dropped through."

Irish looked up. Rose was down on the floor beside Walt. She was crying and saying over and over: "Oh, Walt, you're hurt, you're hurt!"

He said: "I'm all right." Feeling was coming back into his leg. He reached down and felt it and his hand encountered no blood.

Doc Curtis came bustling through the door and poked his ugly face close to Walt's. He opened his bag, adjusted the lantern, and began to cut Walt's shirt away from his shoulder. He straightened a moment later, saying: "Flesh wound. Didn't even tear a muscle. That all? If it is, you'll be OK in a week."

Walt said: "My leg. I don't know."

Doc shifted the lantern again. "Bullet tore hell out of the tip of your holster. Hit a rivet. Let's look at the leg." He straightened then. "The rivet skinned your leg. Impact stunned it, I guess. Come on up to my office where I can tie up that shoulder."

Walt got up a trifle self-consciously. He looked at Rose, then tipped her face and kissed her tear-wet cheeks. "Come on, honey. Let's go home."

A smile came shining through her tears like sunlight shining through a storm. He saw something in her eyes he should have seen many months ago.

Violence had come to Wild Horse Valley, and gone away again. Why it had come, Walt didn't know. But it had cleared old hatreds and jealousies from the air, and, because it had, life could be doubly sweet. Walt slipped an arm around his wife's slim waist and headed for the door.

LAURAN PAINE

❯❯❯❯●◆●❮❮❮❮

GATHERING STORM

The two novels collected in this exciting volume capture perfectly the power and magic of Lauran Paine's work. His characters come alive, his plots create suspense, and his descriptions of the Old West are second to none. The title character in *The Calexico Kid* is a bandit who remains a mystery. Even those who have seen him cannot agree on what he looks like. How, then, can anyone bring him to justice? In *Gathering Storm*, two gunfighters arrive in a quiet range town within minutes of each other. One gunfighter in town is bad enough, but two can only mean trouble. Deadly trouble.